Deadly Predicament

Peter J. Michael

Deadly Predicament

ISBN-13: 978-1-923666-34-4

Published by Peter J. Michael

ALL BOOKS BY THIS AUTHOR ARE:

THE GREAT WAR AGAINST TERRORISM

KILLING THE BOGEYMAN I & II

RUTHLESS

RELIGIOUS DEATH TRAP

THE GOD OF ELIMINATION

THE MURDEROUS MR. A

MADMAN'S RETURN

MURDER AND HOMICIDE I - X

DEADLY PREDICAMENT

Deadly Predicament is a new title sequel expanding the Murder and Homicide cops versus villains' fiction book series.

Deadly Predicament

DEADLY PREDICAMENT

CHAPTER 1

'Day of Retribution'.

Robert Stewart prepared for a period of great and intense violence and bloodshed to hit the streets of New York City. Robert Stewart used his scientific mind in conjunction with mathematical calculations, to forecast and predict the masses of targets his notoriously deranged and heinously bitter adversary Domenico Armando, would be orchestrating the downfalls and destructions of inside his very large and personally handwritten Death List.

Not only had Robert Stewart mathematically calculated the numbers of deaths maniac Domenico Armando planned to commit inside the borders of New York City, but Robert Stewart had also scientifically estimated the sole reasons and dire motivations behind Domenico Armando's soon-to-be unleashed bloodletting sprees. Robert Stewart surely prepared for hell on earth to be let loose without restraints on the streets of New York City - and he knew exactly who the targets were. Domenico Armando planned for a very gory and bloodstained series of corpses to be filling the streets of the entire state of New York at this very moment. Domenico Armando wanted those targets he hated, targets who he blamed for the deaths of his children, to become a profuse blood and slaughter of terrorism-type brutal cruelty inflictions to be used as an example in society of what happens when anyone dares fuck with the Armando Family Empire and the Armando family heirs.

Domenico Armando wanted the blood-soaked corpses of his targets to be lying publicly and quite visibly by all passersby on the streets of the entire state. Domenico Armando insisted that all his enemies be slaughtered, assassinated in a very callous and grossly horrifying, disgustingly violent manner, so that their bodies would be easily identified by everyone in the city and state, especially law enforcement, as an example of how justice should be performed against such evil and wicked coward fucking scumbags he labelled, the very scum who brazenly participated in the deaths of his much beloved children. Domenico wanted those targets murdered and their bodies found completely smeared with blood, full stop! Domenico Armando would commence in the mass assassinations immediately. And Robert Stewart understood that New York City would certainly become a bloody battle marked by the shedding of red blood, via the gory, monstrously violent killing field endless slaughters of all those Domenico Armando deemed responsible for crossing his family's inheritors and descendants!!!

Robert Stewart already dictated the long list of targets in his mind, before he filed all the targets, he had personally written down himself inside police headquarters, he forecasted his enemy would be hunting down and liquidating at once. Robert Stewart not only identified the extensive mass numbers of targets Domenico Armando wanted massacred, but Robert Stewart also pinpointed the exact reasons as to why Domenico Armando wanted such people assassinated at once, the wickedly monstrous motivations!!!

And these were the precise detailed lists of targets Robert Stewart filed inside police headquarters, he accurately ascertained in himself Domenico Armando was currently gunning for, with a viciously ferocious tyranny and equally barbaric bloody-minded nastiness. The targets Robert Stewart cleverly estimated who had their lives hanging in the balance at this very moment were as follows: politicians, priests, teachers, doctors, nurses, psychiatrists, psychologists, publishing criminals and even judges!

And Robert Stewart of course understood the very justifications, the cold-blooded motivations behind the conspiracy to systematically slaughter all such suspected targets.

In Domenico Armando's mind, all politicians were corrupt. 'Those fucking bastard criminals all deserve to die!' Domenico Armando would constantly insist to his extensive manpower of expert killer assassins within his family empire's army regime. 'The politicians are crooked, dirty, nasty, sneaky, high-taxing, high inflation, bribable, corruptible, perverted, underhanded, sold out fucking loathsome scum. They sold out the country and its people a very long time ago! The politicians are only in their jobs for the money, and they are very secretive about their motivations for climbing their posts in high office. The politicians are sadists. Those fucking scum enjoy making people suffer! The politicians have destroyed democracy across the entire world, because they thrive on dehumanising the entire human race! The politicians are dishonest, unethical and depraved! Those fucking scumbags, those immoral twerps and cunts, those gutless motherfuckers are solely out to destroy the people who are stupid enough to vote them into office. The politicians are smiling in front of everybody's faces and promising the people to have their best interests at heart, but truly the politicians are gutless, backbiting, two-faced criminals, and backstabbing schemers and deceivers! The people were stupid enough to vote them in office without knowing that the politicians really want to destroy them! The politicians enjoy legislations which put the entire community of their constituents in deadly harm's way! The politicians are greedy self-serving, self-absorbed malicious bigots! They are narcissistic psychotic and insane, ill-equipped fucking lunatics. The politicians couldn't even run a backyard raffle of anything remotely lucrative, without resulting in losses after losses after losses after fucking losses. Everything they touch, they fuck up and destroy! The politicians couldn't even tie their own fucking shoelaces, so how the hell could anybody remotely think that they are going to run the fucking country? You think they can run anything upwards? I don't fucking think so! All the fucking politicians will do is run the fucking country into the fucking ground! And the proof is in the results.

'They have run the fucking country into the fucking ground. High inflation, high taxes, and unlivable wages, corrupt medical organisations across the entire country and even unaffordable healthcare. They have also been responsible for a criminal-based educational system. All the teachers are criminals; teaching their students to be criminals to rip-off and destroy every member of the community they come into contact with. Look at how the fucking teachers teach their students to become doctors… And witness the horrible incorrect fraudulent teachings of all those stupid idiot politicians who only know how to run the country backwards politically, socially and economically. Students become the worst practitioners and are educated to explore and utilise the worst-case scenario once they leave school, college and university. Everything the so-called educators teach is back-to-front and inside-out! You only need to look at the scum students that come out of university! Once they put the theories of their teachings into practise, so many lives who stumble across their paths end up destroyed. The doctors are killing all their patients. The politicians with their unsurpassed bastardly, maliciousness and evil political divisive anarchy, and nonsensical fucked-in-the-head, moronically retarded legislations, have caused the country politically, socially and economically to go backwards! Can anyone deny that??? The teachers and the stupid politicians they have taught are all responsible for all that goes wrong on all levels of the community. Those teachers have taught the world incorrectness, full stop!!! Will I not punish all the teachers for this? Will I not massacre all teachers brutally, callously, viciously and deservedly for all their evil teachings to their imbecile, gullible and naive students? Of course, I will slaughter the teachers. Of course, I will slaughter their students! Of course, I will slaughter all those who are written in my black book with my own finger for mass terminations!!!

'The repulsive teachers are going to pay. And the repulsive politicians think they're going to get away with their wickedness and evil they have bestowed upon the community and the world at large, punishing the people, starving the community, and robbing every one of their lifeblood monetary savings, necessary opportunities and so forth… No, no, no! You nasty teachers and nasty politicians. The teachers who teach falsehoods and wickedness will be disappearing right under the noses of all their dumb students listening to their gasps of lies and whispers of deceits inside classrooms all over the world, beginning in this country and this city of New York. And of course we cannot forget about the politicians. The politicians are scumbags, PERIOD!!! They are the true rapists and terrorists of the world! Their feeble attempts of running a country is in fact complete anarchy, once the foolish theories of their horrendous belief systems are put into miserable practical assertions, called legislations, within the community, costing the community their lifeblood, their rights to democracy, their rights to affordable and correct education and their rights to affordable and correct health care. The politicians are lining their own pockets like the malignant cancers they are, at the expense of everyone else. The politicians are in fact destroying and murdering the people. The politicians are truly running the whole place into the fucking ground left, right and centre across the entire country!!! Those are the politicians which exist in this world today, in this country - and New York City, and certainly and surely, the entire globe itself. Will I not punish the politicians for their wicked deeds against the people, which has cost them their lives, the same as the politicians and their sick legislations and corrupt, heinously wicked judicial system criminal legislation loopholes, have been responsible in acquitting guilty people, such as those who were responsible for the deaths of my children, as the politicians were responsible for legislating criminal laws, which allowed criminals to wipe out a race and races of people in the community. You politicians will shortly die for your crimes against innocent people, such as those innocent bloodlines of my family tree. And the evil sinful priests are going to die for forgiving all such scum in our society of their crimes. The priests are guilty of performing such sick and disgusting rituals inside their church confessionals on a daily basis!!! ALSO - prepare to be eliminated you filthy, wicked and ignorant priests of the world!

'And of course we cannot forget about the doctors. The scum criminal doctors. The scum wicked doctors, nurses, psychiatrists and psychologists all guilty of torturing and killing their patients for money, big sums of money – and for doing their jobs incompetently, cold-heartedly and downright absolutely unconscionably! Those are the scum fucking doctors we have in this world. Those fucking doctors couldn't even fix a fucking mosquito bite. They couldn't even get rid of a fucking pimple - and those scum doctors are calling themselves 'doctors of medicine'. They think they are doctors of important human organs of the anatomy. The doctors cannot even cure their own insane mental conditions of greed, selfishness, unquestionable immorality and strongly perverted, unreasonable errors of judgement and ignorance in training modules in all forms of the very field of medicine they pretend to be practising and knowledgeable of, in which their evil incorrect practises cause so many of their patients more grief than the original conditions they had first consulted such idiot piece of shit doctors concerning to begin with! The doctors know shit! But, if truth be told, the doctors are careless wicked rapists of people's money and sometimes the doctors are raping people's bodies...the sick, sick scum that the doctors are. The doctors have no morals. The doctors have no ethics. The doctors have no fucking backbone, knowledge and no belief system or inkling or motivation to help any of their patients, full stop! No, no, no, no, no. The doctors are only in the business of smirking at their patients' misfortunes and taking their patients' monies for hurting them furthermore - and stealing their money as they had done with my beautiful, wonderful son, George the Great! And I hereby declare and decree to the entire fucking world of stupid idiots and fucking morons, that the doctors, the nurses, the psychiatrists, the psychologists who practise ill-intentions, wickedness and evil sadism towards their patients, will shortly die torturously at my hands, for all their crimes against those patients that they have been responsible for torturing and killing, as they had been responsible for torturing and killing my wonderful handsome son George the Great! So be prepared to die you sick, demented, criminally insane lunatics, all of you guilty doctors, nurses, psychiatrists and psychologists! Your days of murder and money-stealing lunacy against your patients, is hereby declared over by I-me-Domenico Armando! I will surely slaughter you all this day!'

CHAPTER 2

Robert Stewart also calculated the sickly insane and monstrously destructive and hateful words and conspired actions by his primary genocidal monster target Domenico Armando, against the rest of his declared fair game prey, he vowed to make a complete mockery of, by declaring them all to become sitting ducks to his explosive wrath and equally devastating arsenal directed their way.

'Yes, you publishing criminals. Don't think for a second that I have forgotten about you. For the death of my beautiful daughter Maria, I will truly bring about pain and slaughter against all of your fucking lives! Because you are scum. And you scumbags have failed to abide by rules of integrity towards your customers, your clients, full stop! Yes, indeed. You have done everything wrong and wicked in my eyes! You have done nothing correct, especially when it comes to my beautiful daughter, or should I say, my beautiful dead daughter Maria. Yes. You have certainly performed sins of great evils against all your clients. That is what you fucking cretins are all guilty of committing! You have done nothing right by anybody! No. Not at all! Instead, you have failed everybody because of your jealousy, self-hatred and wicked nastiness! You have run your entire organisations with hate and maliciousness! And for that I will surely obtain my revenge, and I will torture and destroy you all! Because of your pitiful and disgusting jealousies, you publishing criminal fuckheads were driven to plot and scheme behind your customers' backs. You backstabbed your clients and planned to ruin your clients' books through gossip and slander and all forms of sabotage – and you also conspired to not only block your clients' books, but also, through your evil works of deception behind the scenes, you plotted to steal their royalties! For that I will cut your fucking hands off, you thieves. And then I will slaughter you all into the next world, you demonic wicked scums! Yes, you scum publishing criminals are certainly into every unethical business practise anyone can even think of. So, you can surely expect your lives to end immediately, full stop!!! For all that you do, I will make all of you drop dead at once, at once before my feet! You hear me you publishing criminal scums!!! At once I will terminate your fucking lives!

'And of course the judges. Yes. I must make serious mention of the judges of the world! Judicial corruption is everywhere. Corruption in our courts of law is indeed at epidemic proportions all over the globe!! It's so much more apparent than one could possibly realise - and damaging to the fair distribution of court case outcomes! And it is up to me Domenico Armando to combat this sickly judicial corruption which causes a lack of transparency in our independent courtrooms. Evilness within the walls of the justice system and judicial courtroom corruption certainly undermines the necessity in upholding the law with fairness, equality and honourable legislations which otherwise define the rule of law. The judges are all corrupt. The judges and judicial officials continuously misuse their powers inside their courtrooms to give the blameless unfair verdicts and the blameworthy unfair benefits which damages people's lives - and destroys societal foundations, also damaging the psyche of all innocent victims, who were unfortunate enough to step foot inside a disgusting courtroom, facing the judges' evil wicked rulings of unfairness, lies, deceit, manipulation and bias, which certainly ruins societal foundations and erodes public confidence in the judicial process handed down by unfair and wickedly incorrect verdicts, via disgusting immoral judges every day of the wickedly shameful and disgracefully corrupt judicial system's practises! Yes. It is certainly true, that judicial corruption is at epidemic proportions in this world. The judges and courtroom officials involve themselves in gaining illicit benefits via the exploitation of their positions.

'The judges are involved in bribery, favouritism, bias, due to the immoral unlawful undue influence from wealthy and powerful individuals and illegitimate parties! **It is truly sickening!** What goes on inside the courtrooms at all times revolves around lies, manipulation and deceitful legal outcomes which destroys the true fabric of what should be an ordinarily functional legal system! I charge all of you judges with treason. And I will sentence all of you guilty judges to the death penalty, my rules, my expectations, my judgments!!! You judges charged with treasons on all levels, are going to be brought to your knees for your acts of wickedness against the innocent, which have at the same time, caused criminals in our society to flourish, such as those villainous murdering fiends in medicine and the fraudulent, stealing and slanderous fucking cunts operating inside the publishing industry, who were all responsible for the deaths of my children, for sure! Yes. It is you judges truly responsible for acquitting the criminals inside your courts of law and returning them back onto the streets to continue their crimes, as they continued their crimes against people such as my children! Yes, they certainly had. Yes, for sure. Yes, indeed, I decree they are all guilty. Just like you judges who failed to punish the wicked inside your courts of law! You hear me, you scum judges? You are responsible for keeping criminals on the streets, and those criminals such as those in the publishing industry and those in medicine were responsible for killing my children! You deceitful judges have substantially increased the corruption hazards and evil risks perpetuated daily inside your courtrooms! Because you judges are greedy. You spend your salaries on exorbitant resources and in turn, you sell your souls to the devil! You take bribes and you swing both sides of the fence to pervert judicial outcomes and acquit the guilty.

'You filthy judges punish the innocent, and you reward the guilty with unjust verdicts. You do all this, you dirty scum judges, all for money! I will certainly make all of you notoriously criminal judges and courtroom officials extinct from the earth, for your evil wickedness you continuously practise as judges and courtroom officials on a daily fucking basis, you ignorant, disgusting and contemptible judicial system operators of immoralities and unethical, morally depraved sick lunacies! I will make you judges extinct for sure. You are going to drown in a sea of blood I spill from your bodies, from every vein of your criminal beings, you evil, sick, wildly foolish, monstrously brutal, irrationally mad, fucking dirty judges! You hear me, you scum judges? You will all die for your courtroom evil practises! You judges have no belief system! You flip-flop on decisions and allow, what should be, a no-nonsense approach and solid foundations to hearings, trials and final court case outcomes to change unpredictably. What should be firm beliefs, turn, change and switch up at a moment's notice to beliefs of movable sand. You are very fickle you scum judges. You will acquit the guilty at only a simple whim if it suits your purpose, you filthy judges. And because of your money-hungry greed, you certainly created opportunities for corrupt shortcuts in the judicial system's courts of law! You have certainly taken a backseat to transparency and accountability. Because of the existence of so many unethically wicked, morally bankrupt and sinisterly corrupt judges, you allow criminals to delight in unfair court case outcomes favouring them, and you have created unethical behaviour to flourish without detection inside your courtrooms!

'Because of you wicked judges, there is no judicial integrity in existence throughout the world's courtroom practises! Yes. The judges have committed wickedness inside their courtrooms left and right! The judges have corrupted the entire justice system on all angles, simply motivated by acts of bias and monetary greed. Who can have confidence in the judicial system anywhere in the world? Of course, no one. This is a shameful act. And because of such twisted-and-deliberate violations to moral values, I have to decree that every judge in the entire universe must be marked for death, because the judges are not what the judges are supposed to be. Instead of the judges' ruling with integrity, the judges have all gone rogue. The judges are guilty of lies and manipulation and falsifying records just for the sake of earning an extra dollar in their greedy pockets! The judges are the scum of the earth! But where do you think you're going to go you scum judges? I tell you where you are headed you vermin judges…and that is straight into the local cemetery, after I first open up your veins and drain you of the lifeblood force which fuels your criminal mindsets, that lack integrity and forthrightness to act honestly and fairly inside your courtrooms. So, prepare to die you evil judges, full stop! Prepare to be butchered to death, you deranged charlatan judges and criminally insane courtroom officials!!! This is certainly a profoundly sick society with very sick people occupying its boundaries. And the world has the audacity to say that I-me-Domenico Armando is a crazy insane homicidal tyrant. Am I the genocidal monster or is it all of you scums who are false prophets, who appear harmless, but are all venomous snakes, hiding behind fancy titles calling yourselves politicians, priests, teachers, publishing proprietors, judges, doctors, nurses, psychiatrists, psychologists, and all forms of pretentious titles you dare label yourselves with? Indeed.

'You can fool the world you fake, phoney, pretentious, malicious creeps, but can you fool Domenico Armando? Of course not! You can fool the entire people, but I am the one you can never fool! And for your insidious crimes, your death sentences will begin at this very moment, because you cannot trick or deceive me-Domenico Armando. So, prepare to die all of you evildoers and pretentious swindlers. You are all scam artist frauds, unconvincing in anything real, but try-hard degenerates, perverted vile slime, two-faced filthy parasites, little worms, sewer rats floating in the shit below.

'Your egos are awful and foul, shit just like your lack of characters, you evil politicians, you evil priests, you evil teachers, you evil doctors, you evil nurses, you evil psychiatrists, you evil psychologists, you evil publishing criminals and you evil judges of society in general! Get ready all of you targets of mine. Get ready for death. Because I-me-Domenico Armando is coming after you. I'm hunting you all down. I'm going to drag you by your arses out into the open, and you will become sitting ducks to my armies, my hired assassins, who will use you as target practise and slaughter you all into the streets and spill your blood. Yes. Truly! Truly! That is certainly how it will all unfold. So, right now, I hereby declare that New York City will indeed become a river of blood by all the villainous, jealous, thieving, stealing, good-for-nothing, worthless stink bomb faecal matter bums occupying this community on all levels. So do not wake up in the morning feeling like you have benefited monetarily by the deaths of my children. No one of you has benefited from anything. Because I will slaughter you all only after I have brutally tortured you. And this is how I am going to torture you… I will drag you out into the streets and publicly have you bashed. I will also have you whipped naked in the streets, to be humiliated before the entire community by my killer armies, before my soldiers open their machine guns and slaughter you like the dogs and the swine that you are. Yes. In the streets in front of everyone will I humiliate you. Yes. I will slaughter you all in the streets in front of everyone. But you will be first bashed painfully, and like the sick animals you are, you will then be whipped with steel chains and many strokes of a strap and rod. I will break your bones first before having you all machine-gunned down dead like the animals you are. Yes. You will all be dead into the streets, you scum, you swine, you vermin trash!!!'

CHAPTER 3

Robert Stewart could ascertain the very irony in the dire situation at present. Because it was Commander Robert Stewart himself who also targeted the very criminals in society which became the sought-after and wanted prey by his greatest enemy in the world Domenico Armando. It was just a question of timing for both parties concerned. And the further greatest question in the equation was, who was going to get those predators first? Was it Commander Robert Stewart of the 25th division precinct station house in Brooklyn, New York, or was the truly defined genocidal monster and crazy insane homicidal tyrant of New York City and New York State, called Domenico Armando? It was really only a question of who was 'first' going to capture and remove all those corrupt members of society being targeted by both Robert Stewart and Domenico Armando at the same time in September 1998!!!

Robert Stewart had spent the past few weeks investigating and arresting more corrupt judges, corrupt doctors, corrupt pharmacists in ongoing police investigations that unearthed horrendous displays of misconduct and criminal behaviours within the medical fields and judicial system. These criminals knew that they were currently being targeted by both Robert Stewart and Domenico Armando. And it was most certainly a question of who would get them first!

And throughout his police investigation(s), Commander Robert Stewart identified extensive political corruption within the vicinity of New York City, which involved the protection of a Big Pharma Chief Executive Officer.

New York City was certainly no stranger to political corruption. And in the past, many journalists wrote numerous stories and articles to this effect in the aftermath of extensive police investigations, once exclusive stories had been uncovered to them. Headlines such as: Why Is There So Much Political Corruption In New York City? Why Are New York Politicians So dirty - and The Community Is Sick And Tired Of Political Corruption In New York, began circulating the rounds! And now Robert Stewart had painted an extremely horrible picture of potential corruption at the highest levels of state government in New York City, which reached the door to the state's governor himself. Robert Stewart began his investigation extensively into medical corruption which uncovered a Big Pharma Boss in New York City. And this investigation also linked the New York City Governor also being accused of fraud and an extensive cover-up, through receiving gifts by a Big Pharma CEO, in order to conceal and disguise very diabolical crimes linked to the dangers of specific manufactured drugs, which in fact had caused extensive organ damage to patients prescribed such deadly medications, that were supposed to be used to treat very serious human medical conditions. And the New York City Governor was receiving gifts and payoffs by this Big Pharma Chief Executive in New York to cover it all up.

The unravelling of the truth into the investigation beginning with Big Pharma was quite sickening to law enforcement officers. Big Pharma had made false beliefs and false claims about the medications they were manufacturing, which surely contributed to the staggering numbers of loss of life. Even legitimate doctors were being manipulated that such medications they were given to prescribe to their patients would help the sick. But the medications had surely led to the deaths of their patients. Robert Stewart's investigations into medical corruption found that some doctors were legitimate and thus became alarmed at the results of deaths against their patients. But at the same time, other doctors were hideously corrupt and did not care if the drugs killed their patients. It was those knowing criminal doctors that Robert Stewart was after and had been targeting for arrest and prosecution during this current period of police investigations into blatant medical corruption in the city! Also, the pharmacists knew that the medications they were dispensing to doctors' patients were rather deadly - and henceforth, the careless, negligent and fraudulent pharmacists were not warning the patients to the dangers of the prescription medications to all those sick individuals entering their pharmacies across the entire city and state of New York. False beliefs were being manipulated about certain medications. Deadly drugs were being described by Big Pharma and many pharmacists as safe, opposite to the truth, only motivated for the commercialization of ill-founded medical knowledge, rather than the truth coming out into the open, based on actual scientific data into the deadly drugs, and the risky side effects they had in fact caused to so many people who had been prescribed to take into their systems such lethal drugs.

In accordance to all this information coming to the surface, Robert Stewart's investigation at this period of time had revealed the corruption of a very insidious Big Pharma Chief Executive Officer in New York City, a handful of corrupt pharmacists and many corrupt doctors in the area, all on the fix, to blind the truth that certain drugs were killing their patients and not as they actually were being advertised, quite falsely, as life-saving drugs.

Robert Stewart intensified his investigation into medical corruption now targeting the specific Big Pharma CEO in New York in question, and the governor of the State protecting this Big Pharma Chief Executive Officer for perks, gifts and bribes. Big Pharma, the governor of New York, doctors and pharmacists were manipulating truths and covering up deathtrap facts, that certain drugs being manufactured and prescribed to sick patients would result in them dying quicker. And these manipulated truths were intended for the sole purpose of making money, large amounts of money by all parties involved. Now the major cover-up was being unearthed by Robert Stewart and the New York City Police Department.

Robert Stewart not only investigated patient deaths by doctors, including the dispensing of deadly drugs by knowing pharmacists across the city, but his investigation into medical corruption had suddenly reached the doorsteps of a very major criminal Big Pharma CEO in New York, who was being protected by a very corrupt politician right at the top seat of politics in the State, who was none other than the governor himself!

Robert Stewart began his intensified police investigation at present by questioning certain legitimate doctors and pharmaceutical executives, who had no problem exposing systematic corruption and the concealment of the truth by this Big Pharma CEO in New York, who ran his company for the sole purpose of money-making endeavours, prioritising financial gain over public health. Certain doctors and several pharmaceutical executives gave their testimonies rather forthrightly to Robert Stewart and his police investigators, which revealed that this horrendous Middle Eastern Big Pharma CEO situated in New York City, was only in the business of manufacturing dangerous drugs for the sole purpose of making large sums of money, by concealing the dangerous side effects in diabolical proportions of such drugs given to specific chronically ill patients, through lies, deceptions and manipulating crucial data and scientific analysis and analyses of such drugs, which otherwise revealed that those drugs would certainly end up killing chronically ill patients far quicker than the original chronic conditions the sick patients initially reported and were diagnosed with by numerous doctors across the city. Robert Stewart instantly made the claim inside his police file report of medical corruption, that the Middle Eastern Big Pharma CEO situated in New York City was corrupt, evil and extremely dangerous to every sick patient in the city and state of New York. Thus, the community given access to the deadly drugs meant that this Big Pharma CEO highest-ranking executive of his organisation in New York, was manufacturing and making available to the public certain medications that would kill them quickly!

Robert Stewart would now go after this Big Pharma CEO with increased intensity, especially since his investigation against the specific Middle Eastern Big Pharma CEO in New York, uncovered the diabolical protection racket this Big Pharma Chief Executive was given by the New York Governor himself. The New York Governor was also labelled by Robert at this very moment as not only corrupt, but wickedly evil, who certainly had the people of the entire state's worst interests in mind and in his heart. And this case became a major stepping stone into unravelling political corruption in New York at its worst! Both the Big Pharma Chief Executive Officer and the New York Governor had not only risked but were directly responsible for masses of people's lives being killed because of their selfishness and monetary greed. Robert Stewart not only wanted to **BAN** for life this alleged corrupt Big Pharma Chief Executive Officer from the Pharmaceutical Industry, but he wanted him as well imprisoned for life for wilfully manufacturing deadly drugs which killed masses of people in the city, for the sole purpose of making exorbitant sums of money.

At the same time, Robert Stewart also targeted the very criminal and very corrupt governor of New York, who was accepting hefty payoffs on the side and in secret by this wicked Big Pharma CEO, to protect and conceal the truth, that his manufactured drugs for all forms of diseases, such as diabetes, liver, kidney and heart organs and cancer drugs, did not benefit any of the patients diagnosed with such serious health conditions, but in fact expedited rather rapidly the sudden deaths of all those patients prescribed such deadly drugs manufactured by this very evil, very sick and very money-hungry, greedy Big Pharma Chief Executive Officer in New York City!

The corrupt Big Pharma CEO was established in Queens, New York. And he was a 65-year-old, Middle Eastern descent, chief executive officer born in Iraq - and emigrated to the United States of America in his early twenties, beginning his Pharmaceutical Industry Empire, then based in New York City, over the last ten years. He began his profession as a pharmacist, to pharmacy manager, and then pharmacy owner. He later expanded his scope into pharmaceutical research and development by seeking employment inside Big Pharma, to his current position of ten years as Big Pharma CEO in Queens, whose name was Amir Hamza. He was a stocky-built man with very devious and wicked, black-coloured eyes, very thick wavy black hair, dark skin, who was very well-versed in the bloody ideas of terrorism from his native background and upbringing in Iraq, whose family and friends were connected to several terrorist organisations. Mr. Amir Hamza watched his family and neighbours in Iraq kill and eventually be killed during terrorist acts by opposing enemy forces and opposing armies. So, Amir Hamza, with his background and foresight to selling his soul for money regardless of the consequences, devised the scheme to make plenty of money by escaping the fate of his family and neighbours in Iraq, through simply migrating to the United States of America and beginning an empire in pharmaceutical medicine.

Furthermore, as CEO into research and development of medications, he sought to perform his duties negligently, uncaringly and criminally for the sole purpose of swindling others, manipulating and defrauding the market research of deadly drugs to all consumers dumb and gullible enough to believe the false hype, coming from his own mouth - and secured becoming one of the United States of America's great billionaires, by selling drugs, which eventually were proven to harm people for large sums of money! This Big Pharma Chief Executive called Amir Hamza was one of Big Pharma's dirtiest highest-ranked executives stationed in New York City, who not only contributed to soaring prescription costs to patients, but he was one of the country's dirtiest Big Pharma drug manufacturing executives behind a staggering amount of patient deaths, which caused a plummeting and dwindling trust in the medical pharmaceutical industry at present! In crux, Amir Hamza was raking in millions and millions of dollars in compensation, at the same time as the patients using his manufactured drugs not only struggled the extremely exorbitant costs of drug prices, but in the end they paid the ultimate price, when such drugs they were taking manufactured by Amir Hamza had cost them their lives, because of the very deadly-and-lethal side effects of Amir Hamza's drug manufacturing enterprise. Amir Hamza was Big Pharma's richest of the rich in New York City and the United States of America. Amir Hamza was certainly one of the pharmaceutical industry's Big Titans, but a very evil one at that. And his fraud and the misleading advertisement on his life-threatening deadly drugs certainly turned him into one of the world's billionaires. Amir Hamza was one of healthcare's worst of the worst drug manufacturers.

Amir Hamza was the inventor of many cancer drugs and human organ drugs responsible for countless deaths across the entire country. Amir Hamza promoted his deadly drugs and fabricated the fraudulent and deceptive marketing for such drugs as something they were not. Amir Hamza claimed his drugs were safe, harmless and even lifesaving, but Robert Stewart's current police investigation into Amir Hamza's drug inventions made widely accessible to the entire public community of New York City and the United States of America as a whole, had proven that such drugs were being falsely advertised as something they were not: safe. But in actual fact, the created drugs were proven to be very dangerous, very toxic and very deadly. And Robert Stewart was after Amir Hamza's blood, mixed together with the blood of the diabolically wicked, careless mass murdering tyrant's cover up of the crimes headed by Mr. Governor of New York, who was called Thomas Rogers. The New York Governor Thomas Rogers was also a 65-year-old man, but of American descent, with diabolically shifty brown-coloured eyes, white-coloured straight hair with a side part, medium-built, medium-height - and voted into office with the same misconstrued and deceitful public promotion, that won him governor of the state recently as Amir Hamza earned his billions in his field of pharmaceutical drug creations, under a pretext and pretence of lies, not only sugar-coating, but completely covering up the truth of his evil-and-dangerous attributes to the community, truly earning him the title as one of the world's multibillionaires.

CHAPTER 4

Amir Hamza was a narcissist, megalomaniac, psychopath, sociopath, money-hungry greedy fraud and a mass murderer to all those sick patients across New York City, the United States of America and the world itself, through the numerously risky-and-hazardous drug creations he made available to the public at large. Amir Hamza was all bad with not one good quality to his credit, but he was not completely stupid. He understood what the stakes were all too well! Amir Hamza forecasted the equally dangerous risks headed his way by a certain police commander operating in the city and state of New York, through his recent unpredictable knockout powerful crackdowns made against criminal doctors and criminal pharmacists across the vicinity of the regions. Amir Hamza dreaded the very thought of what Police Commander Robert Stewart stood for.

Robert Stewart was a very determined, very clever and very masterful cop who surely had no equal. Commander Robert Stewart was the name, rank and serial number he suddenly came to know and fear! Amir Hamza read the

English newspapers which stated that not only was Robert Stewart cracking down on medical corruption throughout the city and state of New York, but on top of that, a very sick and very deadly and equally determined tyrant hiding in the city called Domenico Armando was also after settling scores against medical corruption he blamed for the death of his son George the Great. Amir Hamza was painfully aware that he was being targeted on two fronts, both by the Police Commander Robert Stewart and this evil dictator called Domenico Armando!

Amir Hamza sat inside his high-rise office in the Queens Borough of New York, as he contemplated his fate yet filled with confidence and much determined to defeat and outsmart all odds surrounding him at present, as he thought to himself: just try and get me you two fucks. You two foxes and sharks will not get the better of me. I am a terrorist by name and by nature. I'm of Middle Eastern descent and I will stab, shoot and exterminate all threats against me, and I will secure my Kingdom and my billions at the expense of everyone's lives today as I have done in the past in this wretched city and country of the West. I don't care if my drugs are deadly, killing everyone who consumes them. All I do know, is that no one will destroy my company's legacy. I am the CEO and chairman of my pharmaceutical-created legacy, and you two dogs Robert Stewart and sick fuck Domenico Armando will not invade my territory and stop my money-making enterprise ever, ever, fucking ever. I come from a solid-rock foundation. I'm Middle Eastern. Let me repeat: I'm a terrorist by name and a terrorist by nature and I will outfight and outwit the two of you fuckers. None of you will get me but I will get you first. I will prescribe you fuckhead rat blockhead imbecile idiots my deadly drugs – and I will watch you both drop dead at my feet, as everyone else has died from the prescriptions of my created lethal-and-dangerous medications consumed by many!

I will forever remain untouched by you Commander Robert Stewart and you devil Domenico Armando. So, the two of you can go fuck yourselves and both kill each other, because you will be unsuccessful in killing me!

Commander Robert Stewart identified quite clearly that Big Pharma fish such as Amir Hamza had behaved much like a pack of sharks, swallowing up other rival pharmaceutical industry rivals, orchestrating elaborate acquisition deals to remain on top of the pharmaceutical industry's food chain, taking advantage of such rivals' weaknesses as Big Pharma Shark Amir Hamza looked to such targets to gobble them up in forced merger deals, totally resembling a deadly drug-manufacturing, unsafe drug-creating predator.

Amir Hamza was a very greedy, self-serving, self-entitled beggar of a man, who did not just want to create a multi-billionaire enterprise in the pharmaceutical industry, but he also wanted to steal and takeover other drug manufacturing companies and amalgamate them into his own enterprise. Thus, he looked to all rival targets locally and even abroad to take over their businesses and incorporate them into his own Queens drug industry, to continue the Amir Hamza bloodline as the wealthiest filthy rich shareholder in the pharmaceutical industry across the world! Amir Hamza's invented drugs branched into developments for breast cancer, heart disease, liver, kidney and brain disease medications, as well as so-called treatments for a variety of terminal cancers throughout the head and body. But what was not exposed until this very moment was that all his drugs for all types of organic and cancerous treatments were extremely deadly in their natures - and had in fact been responsible for claiming the lives and notoriously killing a multitude of people not only throughout the United States of America, but throughout the world itself such drugs were made available to, via many other merged pharmaceutical companies Amir Hamza had taken over in recent years, as the greedy shark predator he was renowned to be across the globe.

Amir Hamza was in fact responsible for claiming more deaths than every terrorist leader (he claimed himself to favour and live by such terroristic rules and codes), all combined, over the past thirty years. Amir Hamza was certainly one extremely nasty piece of work that Robert Stewart wanted to expose and nail to the wall with every fibre of his being at present!

Amir Hamza's Big Pharma chain was certainly one of the most corrupt organisations currently residing in practice in the United States of America. Amir Hamza's pharmaceutical drug-making empire was certainly responsible for killing more human lives than the worst terrorist leaders across the world had claimed all combined over the past thirty years! Robert Stewart was definitely and absolutely targeting this evil wicked man with every police resource and all his law enforcement tools and ammunition at his disposal, to put an end to Amir Hamza's mass murdering criminal regime he operated, that was disguised as life-saving drugs to the world, but in truth, this man was a genocidal terrorist and a real-life mass murdering homicidal maniac at large in the city of New York.

Amir Hamza made no bones to the extensive capabilities of this masterful cop named Commander Robert Stewart right now pitted against him, as Mr. Amir Hamza seated himself inside his sky-rise office of a tall building featuring multiple floors in Queens, contemplating the forecasted attacks to be driven his way by Commander Robert Stewart.

Amir Hamza understood Robert Stewart was currently working to eliminate medical corruption in the city of New York. And Amir Hamza knew that Robert Stewart was clever enough to pinpoint him as responsible for the manufacture and creation of deadly drugs at a very high price tag, for both him-Hamza and the medical corrupt industry, to profit big dollars at the expense of human lives.

Amir Hamza drank his expensive wine and was eating his expensive lunch of imported lobster with his fork at present, filling his guts and quenching his thirst, as he considered nothing was too great an expense for him. At the same time as he stuffed his guts, he flicked his thoughts from his food directly to

Commander Robert Stewart – and that police officer's currently predicted forcefully chaotic attacks soon-to-be unleashed against him.

Amir Hamza was a diabolical mass murderer within his pharmaceutical industry, but he was quite clever in psychological diagnosis and personality analysis, and he in fact sought to read Robert Stewart's mind, based on his deductions of his opponent's mindset characteristics at present much driven against him, as he equally sensed the commander's dissection and investigation of him concurrently. Amir Hamza knew Robert Stewart's thoughts. This is what he deduced Robert Stewart was thinking and quite accurately at that, as the police master kept the pharmaceutical industry fraud on his radar: It takes a gutless coward like you Amir Hamza to target the sick and the defenceless across this world with your deadly drugs, motivated only to make large sums of money at their expense and deaths. You thought that your money gave you power Amir Hamza to do as you wanted when you entered the United States with a black heart and sick-minded intentions. You are truly a coward Amir Hamza. My intention is as such: to stop and destroy you, Amir Hamza. I'm going to end your criminal Big Pharma drug-manufacturing death trap you have in store for the world. I'm going to end you, Amir Hamza. I'm going to finish you, Amir Hamza! You are gone Amir Hamza! You are dead!

You made many people suffer and you made many people die throughout the course of the lunacy you practised inside the pharmaceutical industry over the years! You have killed much like the gutless coward that you are Amir Hamza, in the shadows, hiding your true intentions to make money through the mass executions of a staggering number of many people. You will pay Amir Hamza for all of that! I am going to expose you Amir Hamza and then I am going to prosecute you, Amir Hamza. Then, I am going to destroy everything you have and I'm going to destroy you, Amir Hamza!

You will not get away with stealing all the money from your victims and stealing their lives via the creation and availability to the public such deadly drugs, which has surely resulted in claiming thousands, millions, with the intention of killing billions of people across the world. You are one of the worst criminals that I have been forced to target inside my police station office Amir Hamza. You are a true evil and sick sadistic despicable and disgusting nasty piece of work. I am going to destroy you, Amir Hamza. Do you know that your days are numbered Hamza? Can you feel Mr. Amir Hamza that I am coming after you?

Do not worry Mr. Hamza. I know what you are thinking Amir Hamza. You are a coward! I know how you medical cowards and dictators operate. I know you're going to plan to stop me. I know how your sick, gutless mind operates. You are going to send all the medical criminals in New York to come after me and gang up on me like the coward that you are. You cannot come after me on your own, can you Amir Hamza? No, of course not! Because you are a coward. You are going to send many people to come after me, to stop my investigations against you. But let me tell you something Amir Hamza. You are going to fail! You are going to lose! I will crush and destroy you, Amir Hamza!!! Yes. I, Commander Robert Stewart of the 25th division precinct station house of Brooklyn, New York is surely going to send you to your knees Amir Hamza, for your wicked and evil, sick and sadistic crimes you have unleashed across the globe. I will end your tyranny inside the medical industry which has resulted in the deaths and destructions of millions of people around the world Amir Hamza. I am ready for you Amir Hamza. I am ready for you, and I will get you first before you and your gang of medical cowards can try to encircle me and stab me with your syringes, filled with your deadly created drugs.

I know what you are planning Amir Hamza. I can read you like a very diabolically sick book Amir Hamza. But believe me Amir Hamza, my mind is scanning and interpreting your sick mind and your sick thoughts! I know what you are thinking Amir Hamza. I know what you are planning Amir Hamza. But I'm going to get you first Amir Hamza. You will not win victory against me Amir Hamza. I'm going to eliminate you and terminate you and your criminal regime before you ever get a chance to stop me and my investigations against you, Amir Hamza. I will win this war between us Amir Hamza! I'm coming for you Amir Hamza. I am gunning for you Amir Hamza! I have my sights set on you Amir Hamza and I am not going to stop until I utilise every police resource at my disposal to send you to your knees Amir Hamza. And I will send you barking like the dirty dog that you are Amir Hamza to your much-awaited, much-anticipated and well-deserved death and extinction Amir Hamza! I am Commander Robert Stewart of the New York City Police Department, and I declare that your end is coming thick and fast Amir Hamza. I will not stop until you are finished and into the ground

Amir Hamza, for all your mass murdering crimes against your victims in New York, throughout the United States and across the entire world Amir Hamza! You are a black-hearted shark Amir Hamza! You are a diabolical, destructive coward of monumental terroristic proportions - and I will be the death of you Mr. Amir Hamza. That is my decree. That is my declaration against you Amir Hamza.

So, you certainly had better be prepared to face the music and pay the piper for your mass murdering crimes against the sick and the defenceless Amir Hamza. Because I am going to get you before you can get me, you scum of all scums, Amir Hamza! My intention is to make you very sad and to blow your entire world apart with you in it, Mr. Amir Hamza! Yes. I will make you very sad! You are a coward Amir Hamza - and I, Commander Robert Stewart will most certainly prove that even as you and your criminal medical networks are united against me, you still will have no chance of winning against me Amir Hamza!!! You think you are plotting against me Amir Hamza? But what you don't realise is that you are really plotting your own downfall!!!

CHAPTER 5

Amir Hamza understood the stakes were higher than ever around him at present. He knew he was facing a detrimental predicament of kill or be killed. To kill and destroy his target right now was a definite must in himself for his own survival; it was a desperate plot and another desperate plan to secure his continuing legacy of making money via the deaths of sick patients. Amir Hamza was on a rollercoaster ride to neutralise one specific police officer in question called Commander Robert Stewart, before this very viciously determined and genius-like master law-enforcement official titled, Commander Robert Stewart, in simple terms, does him in and puts him into the grave once and for all.

Amir Hamza continued his mindless but deadly furious brainstorm into his current condition and the source of that in himself, equivalent terminal cancer problematic situation, now unleashed upon him and his empire who went by the name of Commander Robert Stewart. He finished his expensive lunch and his expensive bottle of wine sitting on his desk inside his high-rise office building all alone now, contemplating his monstrously evil thoughts and conspired actions within himself. I'm no fool, Commander Robert Stewart. I know what I'm facing. I fear your presence around me; the invisible threatening presence of yours is as suffocating as a secure prison chamber devoid of all oxygen. This is more than just a psychological thriller between us. This predicament is in fact deadly as hell, this, as you Americans call, rock and roll show. We will rock and roll Commander Robert Stewart. I will teach you a Middle Eastern dance as I play my flute and watch you move your legs at my rhythm, much like the snake you are, Commander Robert Stewart. And you will move your legs as I surround you with my medical criminals, all armed with syringes filled with the deadly drugs I have created, pointing those syringes at you. And stabbing them towards you, as I watch you move up and down, dodging the insertions into your body parts to poison you swiftly and accurately until I erase you out of my life, Commander Robert Stewart! But I have to admit Commander Robert Stewart, your presence does make me nervous. For the first time in my life, I'm very nervous. I know of your handiwork and in myself, I fear it. I fear your destructive presence heading my way.

I cannot pretend anymore to stay calm. I cannot remain calm any longer because of you Commander Robert Stewart. I feel my eyes are betraying me. My mind and my thoughts have become treason to my very being. If I continue to remain calm, I will continue to be trying myself. Because of you Commander Robert Stewart, I am now in panic mode. Yes, indeed, Commander Robert Stewart. My eyes are flicking back-and-forth, up and down, searching this room, looking outside the blinds of my top-story office building into the street, looking everywhere into the daylight hours and into the night sky… Yes, I am looking for something invisible and that invisible person targeting me is you Commander Robert Stewart. I am certainly very apprehensive and very nervous at present. That is most definitely a very bad sign for me, signifying something about the way you move and the way you conduct your police investigations, that isn't normal. No! Surely not normal at all! You float through the city much like a ghost, and what takes other investigators years to accomplish, you secure victory against your prey before a lion can roar his ugly teeth just twice when provoked.

You are certainly an enigma Robert Stewart. I know how you operate. I have read how you operate and eliminate your targets as quickly as an exterminator disposes of bodies. Yes, Robert Stewart. Your investigations do not feel casual. No, not at all! Your approach does not seem simple! It feels heavy! Heavy and invisible. Your ghostlike invisibility is performed rather shrewdly. Some may say it is still apparent! I don't know if everyone experiences that. But your presence is still felt, and it definitely feels heavy. I feel heaviness in my chest. I feel heaviness in the atmosphere around me. I know you are targeting me. I know you are somewhere around me, but I cannot see you. Where are you, you devilish ghost? Come out!!! Show yourself to me. Take me out of my misery! Are you watching me? Are you around me right now? Where are you, Commander Robert Stewart? I cannot see you, Commander Robert Stewart. Show yourself to me. Can't you see I am in despair right now? From a very tough mass murdering terrorist, you have reduced me to breadcrumbs of fragility and isolation. You have taken away my strength Robert Stewart. But I must compose myself.

I must gang up on you as I must kill you with my deadly drug creations, before you come anywhere near me with your badge and with your gun and blow my head off

Commander Robert Stewart. I must finagle a way out of this mess you have put me in, Commander Robert Stewart! Because all of a sudden, I'm feeling very paranoid, as if the existence of your damning invisible presence is surrounding me. I cannot pinpoint exactly what's going on around me, but my feelings are becoming intense. My muscles are feeling cramped and my chest is very tight. That's what terrifies me the most about you Commander Robert Stewart… It is that you have not come to interrogate me. It is the fact that you are not talking to me and yet you are invisibly plotting against me, that is what terrifies the fucking hell out of me the most, than if you barged into my office and began yelling at me accusations of committing this…and accusations of committing that... But I know you're not doing that Commander Robert Stewart. You are too cunning and clever a man to know that interrogating me will just be a waste of breath. Because I would give you no information, full stop. Period. But I know Police Commander Robert Stewart, that you are able to extract more information out of me just through your silence of not talking to me, as opposed to being noisy and yelling at me. You are a truly clever man Commander Robert Stewart. The cleverest detective of them all. I know that.

Yes. Even if I whisper to myself, those whispers will bounce off me and enter your psyche to read my thoughts and planned secret moves ahead of schedule, before I can conspire to collapse you into the abyss.

Tell me something, Commander Robert Stewart... Can you see the future? I would like to know Commander Robert Stewart, because if you can see the future, what does it predict? Does it predict that you will kill me, or does it predict that I will kill you first, so that I can continue my drug-creating hypocrisy and legacy of mass murder against the dummies and the suckers of this world? Which will it be Commander Robert Stewart? Will this Big Pharma tycoon Amir Hamza continue to get away with creating exorbitant money-making lethal drugs which killed people, or will you Commander Robert Stewart finally close in on me and end me once and for all? Maybe it sounds like I'm asking these questions like a joke, but I'm really asking, or should I say, begging for answers to my God, as I prayed to him for answers and guidance of how to extricate myself from this mess that you have caused for me Commander Robert Stewart. Because I know you very well enough to know Commander Robert Stewart, that every investigation you conduct is not just commentary, but it's a goddamn fucking lunatic prophecy of the traction you easily make against your prey, which results in the swift deaths of all those targets who enter the files as names inside your hideous police station office. Yes, Robert Stewart, you are certainly a mystery and an enigma, an invisible destroying ghost. You are all that and much more wrapped in flesh! Unlike others in your field, you do not speak hot air, but your actions are louder than words. And your weapons of war are deadly arms of combat that you strike into people's ribs, until you tear the life out of them! Yes, Robert Stewart. You are certainly a very clever man, and I know you are now dissecting my weaknesses and looking for what mistakes you can find to force me to choke on each and every one of those errors of judgement in my past, my present and conspired future actions!

But don't worry Robert Stewart. I will not make the mistake of what others have made in the past. Because your very presence, your very existence in this city around me has served as a clear and distinct warning of what I need to look for. I know you are reading subtle patterns of my behaviour that I'm simply ignoring. But my dear friend, or enemy, Commander Robert Stewart, believe me, I am forewarned. Yes, Robert Stewart. My fear of your investigations has certainly made my anxiety metastasize at this moment to extremely dangerous levels. And my paranoia is compounding by the second, just merely by your name circling my very dark thoughts even casually! Your existence in this city as my neighbour has certainly created something very lethal inside me. And I mean lethal to me, to my existence, to my very foundation, to my entire continued legacy! Fucking badly Robert Stewart. What the fuck have you done to me? The fear of the unknown is making it hard for me to breathe right now. Will I become another statistic through your investigative eyes, ears and breath, Robert Stewart? Are you going to get me the same way you got everybody else in the past Robert Stewart?

I am Amir Hamza, Big Pharma CEO and multibillionaire, who's gotten away with mass murder in the past in his field of operation. I killed people through the creation of my drugs. I was endorsed by the government. I was seen as running a very legitimate organisation. And I was able to kill people left, right and centre across the entire globe, as if I was given a licence to kill and sanctioned to do it. I could create drugs in the past that could kill people and I still got paid handsomely for it. But now Robert Stewart, now as I look at the newspapers and see all those articles written concerning the medical corruption that you are exposing and running into the ground, all orchestrated via your crackdowns and arrests of medical felons and medical mass murderers left, right, and centre, I know you are coming after me next. I know you are coming after me right now. And I have to tell you something Commander Robert Stewart, even if it is just through telepathy, telepathic communications…and that is Commander Robert Stewart, that I'm a little bit nervous, a little bit scared, anxious, paranoid… I'm getting really fucking breathless right now at the thought of you coming after me and getting me anytime now! I know I can fool the whole world. But around you, my facade is penetrated and my lies end up collapsing and the pretence of my entire pharmaceutical industry empire is going to be exposed and crumbled into the dust by your fucking hands, Commander Robert Stewart!

In the past I could defend myself, full stop. But now, the only defence I have is no fucking defence at all. Because I know where you are concerned Commander Robert Stewart, there are no illusions to your masterful game plan of see-through-the-bullshit-of-everyone you come into contact with. I cannot hide, because I know you will seek. I cannot lie, because I know you will unravel. I cannot kill anymore, without you saying it how it is, that I'm a fucking mass murderer! Even as I play dialogue in my head in secret, that has turned into a death trap because of you Commander Robert Stewart. You can see through my games and read my thoughts as gravity! All I know is that my eyes are continuously flickering left and right, up and down to see where you are Robert Stewart, as I wait and anticipate the floor under my feet collapsing right beneath me.

I wasn't ready for you and your presence Robert Stewart. I wasn't ready for my life to collapse in ruins, nor for my life to even be perceived on your radar, to uncover the truths about me and my empire and what they both really stand for! I wasn't ready for any of it, Commander Robert Stewart! No one else can dissect a snake with such cutting accuracy and precise surgical timing as you, Commander Robert Stewart. Where are you hiding Robert Stewart? I know you are somewhere here waiting, hiding invisibly, exposing me from top to bottom. I know you, Robert Stewart. Every prediction of yours is as cutthroat accurate as a fucking blade stabbed into one's heart! You don't even need a crystal ball. You dissect truths in dark accuracy, as if the whole fucking dirty pile of shit containing all our secrets is piled up in one big ball sitting right in front of you inside your police station office. Even without your presence being seen, you are uncovering all out dirty deep dark secrets much like the extraction of a classified file! And this has nothing to do with fucking luck. You are exposing all of us dirty rotten scumbag criminal mass murdering frauds, fakes, phonies, cunts and fucking arseholes like me, as if it's a magician's trick brought into reality. And that is what unnerves me the most about you Commander Robert Stewart. It's how you do it. There is no word said, nothing spoken. Just uncanny knowing of what people like me are and what we truly stand for, as if it's just shoved into your psyche with no effort, no fucking effort at all… You just solve the patterns by default, without anyone understanding how, why, when! And who can do it like that?

You don't need technology to determine the truth. Technology is only a tool you use for evidence gathering to have our sick arses convicted in a court of law! And you are accomplishing this time and time again, over and over and over again, full stop! And it is the consistency in the results that you obtain against pieces of shit terrorist scum like me over and over again, which is completely defying gravity, defying logic, period!!! Is there any comprehension in physics that can decipher what you do and how you do it time and time again, that unravels and exposes people like me with no word, no warning, when no one else in the entire world is able to do what you can do Commander Robert Stewart? You certainly defy gravity. You certainly defy expectations and manuals of conventional law and order.

Because the way you operate Police Commander Robert Stewart is not what usual police officers are taught to operate inside the Police Academy. You Robert Stewart have revolutionised the scope, the very field of law enforcement to make it something that it never was before! And you did that just by your existence! And that very presence and existence of yours situated inside the very walls of the police station in this city, was effective and efficient in all aspects of criminal convictions, exposures and achieving what convention defied as unable to achieve, and that is true physics into law and order - and the disclosures and revelations and the fundamental unravelling of people like me, who can no longer get away with our crimes because of you being in existence, Commander Robert Stewart.

I mean, exposing one person, OK. Exposing two people, OK, no big deal, full stop. Exposing three or four people in your career, still it's just average. We can sum it up to luck. But when you unravel, expose and eliminate every criminal you set your sights on, you certainly achieve what no man has been able to achieve in your field of law and order before Commander Robert Stewart. And that is utter awe and complete shock. You have managed to turn all your police targets, all your police enemies into a gigantically shocked and speechless audience of yours, just through your uncanny abilities of unravel and make extinct! Unravel and make extinct. And again, unravel and make extinct, full stop! And now I feel my chest still tightening and my breath becoming shallow as I'm waiting for the very same treatment to be done on me as you have done on every other target which landed on your police desk inside police headquarters, Commander Robert Stewart! And that is no fucking joke! No coincidence. All your predictions are accurate! All your premonitions about criminals like me turn to reality. And then…then…then…your mysterious aura strikes against us, when you finally confront us, hitting with such magnitude and velocity that it becomes as earth-shattering as 100 land mines planted in one small room, blowing us up and our criminal worlds so fast, that our entire existences end before anyone can even identify that we have ever lived in this world, targeted by you to begin with! Your metaphors in describing us is still precision. Everything you say about us is proven to be so precise, that it becomes instantly catalogued as evidence!

Inside myself, I say fuck Robert Stewart! Toss him aside and dismiss his efforts against me. But I have to fucking damn well tell you, that it's impossible to do that. Because just by the trembling of my bones and the unsettling of my teeth, through that unexplained action of gravity I'm feeling at present, I'm unable to forget about the name Robert Stewart or his premeditated attacks he has in store for me! Your cutting accuracy into our thoughts, our minds and our actions are as if you are a fly who has landed on to the secret journals containing all our jotted landmark incriminating writings, and just began reading an unravelling surreptitiously, not caring to obtain permission from anyone!!! Now can you wholeheartedly understand my firm desire to dispose of you at once Robert Stewart! Your presence is intolerable! Your existence is fucking damnable! Who can put up with this? We have to get rid of you Robert Stewart! The fact that we don't know what you're going to do to us next is the very sickness that you have planted inside our heads! Are you really a human Robert Stewart? Or are you a fucking phenomenon, something inhuman, something unexplainable that can read the future and can predict patterns with razor-sharp awareness, much to our detriments! You have turned me into an addict Robert Stewart, dissecting your past patterns of behaviours - and trying to cross-reference those patterns with what I currently face at the expense of your destructive hands!

Believe me Robert Stewart, I might be a terrorist, but I certainly believe in your power more than I care to admit. And I know the fear you have instilled in me is just another one of your hilarious acts of cruelty driven against me!

Other people need technology planted left, right and centre. And those people are still struggling to uncover the truth. But you Robert Stewart uncover everything just through some supernatural force, some supernatural unexplainable power that resides within you, that helps you uncover, expose and unravel truths that most certainly have baffled the most seasoned experts with all their so-called academic degrees, Doctor of Philosophy awards and alleged qualifications they have in their arsenal! You Robert Stewart have become a living legend inside the black hearts and dark minds of all those residing across the globe's criminal kingdoms! And all of a sudden, all liars, all manipulators, all thieves, all murderers, all scamming cunts just like me across the entire world stop dead in our tracks and think to ourselves, what if Robert Stewart has us on his radar? What if Robert Stewart already knows what we're doing before we have already learned how to spell his fucking name? And you have managed to render us fearful just by your presence alone Commander Robert Stewart. We are paranoid because we know you have invented the compass that pinpoints directly towards us, dissecting and unravelling into the open doorways to all our dirtiest, darkest, ugliest and incriminating secrets to have us all fucking hanged inside your prison cell, Mr. Sir Commander Robert Stewart. That is the fear you have caused to so many of us, Commander Robert Stewart! You are the anatomy, the fucking embodiment of truth dissection and the unforgettable name that renders no mask to remain unpenetrated, no lies remain hidden and no criminal mastermind gets away with anything ever, ever, ever, ever, ever!

And even if we want to adjust our behaviours and censor ourselves, we cannot.

Because we know you would see through all facades of pretence and deception of all us criminals, simply because you have hacked our psychology - and uncovered all out dirty secrets with foresight, some mysterious magic and unmistakable truth serum that you have managed to have cast into all our souls, revealing all that you need to know against us, rendering us in a paralytic state, so we can never ever manage to keep any dark secret from you ever! Your existence Commander Robert Stewart has truly shifted the balance of control. The Criminal Kingdom is no longer in authority. But all elements of the Criminal Kingdom are in fact sweating blood and shaking in fear of what failure to their plans is headed their way - and what earth-shattering catastrophe awaits them by what you have predicted every time you look into our futures!

From certainty, your existence has turned to panic for all of us evildoers! From getting away with our lies, you have turned to incriminating truths. From freedom of operation, you have turned to systematic slaughter inside your death house you call the electric chair, for all of us criminals! You have certainly struck fear into our hearts!

And that is why I must confer at once with my partner in crime, the New York

Governor Thomas Rogers. We must pool our resources and put our minds together, to come up with the one effective solution of how to get rid of you Robert Stewart once and for all, before you do us all in. Because indeed, yes indeed Commander Robert Stewart, you are a dangerous force to contend with. You are too dangerous to be left unattended any further!

Yes, indeed Commander Robert Stewart. You are extremely dangerous to us all, every dirty criminal who lives and breathes, you are a deadly and dangerous threat to us all because of what you know!!!

CHAPTER 6

Robert Stewart's profession as a New York City Police Department professional police officer was tied in with the unpredictable without a moment's notice. Robert Stewart found himself at midnight rushing to the New York governor's official home and residence at the New York State Executive Mansion located at 138 Eagle Street in Albany, New York, responding immediately to a plea for help concerning a serious case of domestic abuse and domestic violence, perpetrated by the New York Governor Thomas Rogers himself against his 49-year-old wife Stacy.

Stacy Rogers was in the middle of being threatened by her husband Thomas Rogers, the New York Governor himself verbally and physically, who not only was abusing her with threatening words, but also the governor struck her physically and violently with his hands. Robert Stewart received the call promptly by Stacy Rogers inside his police station office at midnight, spoke to Stacy Rogers after she was verbally abused and violently beaten by her husband, the governor of New York, and Robert left the station house and entered inside his civilian vehicle at once and headed to the New York State Executive Mansion in Albany to deal with the matter promptly!

As Robert Stewart stormed the governor's residence through the front doors inside the private study room where the violent altercation between Governor Thomas Rogers and his wife was taking place, Robert found that the New York Governor was in the middle of threatening to beat his wife once again.

Robert Stewart received the call from Stacy Rogers earlier in the AM hours, concerning the case of domestic abuse and domestic violence, from the trembling and frightened governor's wife at the 25th division precinct station house in Brooklyn, New York. Stacy Rogers called him in the dead of night, reporting her governor husband Thomas Rogers had been abusing and beating her, because she wanted a divorce, simply because she realised her husband was a terrible man and an immoral human being - and of course her husband would not allow nor tolerate the scandal of a political divorce, more concerned with what bad publicity such a divorce would entail and cause him as governor of the state of New York. So instead of granting his wife what she wanted, a divorce, he began threatening, insulting and beating her senseless into strict obedience, or so he thought that was the result of his volatile mistreatment of his wife Stacy Rogers!

Thomas Rogers considered his brunette wife yet to be quite appealing after twenty years of marriage. And in himself, he would not allow her to have a divorce, nor allow any other man to touch her, as well as tolerate the disastrous scandal and any other horrendous repercussions against him, as a high-ranked politician of New York, following a divorce, that could cost him any upcoming future re-elections in office! So, Thomas Rogers, within his dark and diabolical mindset, and for the sole purpose to contain the quite risky situation, through total control of his wife, and that included verbally and physically threatening, abusing and beating her into submission, the result was deemed to send her to become his then 'forced' spouse.

Her call to Robert Stewart that evening would definitely prove to change things for her for the better. Robert Stewart would free her from her husband and from this catastrophically suffocating marriage she was currently subjected to, much experienced to her shocking dismay, by the very hands of Governor Thomas Rogers.

Prior the telephone call to Robert Stewart at the station house that evening, the governor had finished beating and abusing his wife. And once the governor overheard his wife's phone call to Robert, he attempted to beat her up some more, not only with his hands across her face, but this time he furiously removed from around his waist his black-coloured thick leather belt, and folded it double, and raised his hand threatening to strike his wife with it many times, when Robert Stewart barged inside the house and confronted the diabolical governor, forcing him to stop.

Robert Stewart rushed himself inside the house passed the governor's servants and security detail, entered the study on the other side of the residence and caught the governor in the act of striking his wife with the belt in his hands, he folded in double, ready to attack her with. Robert Stewart instantly raised his voice authoritatively to the governor, shouting the following words to him: "Touch her and I'll tear your arm off!!!"

The governor instantly released his wife, and Stacy Rogers ran towards Robert for protection. Robert asked her if she wanted to press charges against her husband? She responded that she just wanted Robert to take her to a hotel safely away from her husband.

She explained that the way the justice system operated, and the fact that her husband could pay off judges, finalised her firm decision in that matter instantly. And that was not in the affirmative! She responded to Robert that she wouldn't waste her time taking her husband inside a courtroom. So, Robert instantly had escorted the governor's wife Stacy Rogers out of the New York State Executive Mansion in Albany and had transported her to a safe destination far away from her husband.

But before he did exit the building with Stacy Rogers, Robert Stewart pointed his finger threateningly towards Governor Thomas Rogers and demanded to him through saying the following words, at the same time as he stared at him almost dangerously cold, and his voice equally cold as death: "I'm going to take your wife Stacy out of this residence of yours Governor Rogers, but if I find that you try to go anywhere near her or threaten her ever again, I am going to personally bring the world crashing down on top of you - and I will crush you Thomas Rogers right inside this goddamn New York State Executive Mansion that you are currently living in right here and right now! And I don't give a damn who you think you are. Because governor or no governor, I am going to turn your life into a living hell if you disobey my orders and go anywhere near your wife ever again, threatening her verbally or physically!!!"

New York Governor Thomas Rogers understood the solidly strong, explosive and unbendable warning by the great and powerful Police Commander Robert Stewart, full stop! And from this moment on, New York Governor Thomas Rogers realised that his wife Stacy Rogers was completely off-limits to him!

CHAPTER 7

New York Governor Thomas Rogers was unable to sleep at all that night. His mind was preoccupied in immense worry and fear over one man, one name, one title - and that was Commander Robert Stewart. That fucking crazy cop is going to be the death of me! He kept thinking to himself. Because of the existence of that bastard antagonistic cop Commander Robert Stewart, I will never be able to sleep again! He even lost his appetite for breakfast. He usually ate a big hearty breakfast whipped up nicely by his chefs and hand-delivered to him personally inside his executive mansion by his maids and servants. But the next morning, when he woke up at 6:00 AM, he alerted his staff, chefs and assistant cooks to not prepare him anything special that morning, just to give him one simple cup of coffee. He would not explain details to his staff, but only said that all of a sudden, he lost his appetite for the first time in his life! In himself, in his mind, Governor Thomas Rogers wondered if Robert Stewart had cost him his appetite for the rest of his life on this earth, as well as his sanity and peace of mind, suddenly being ripped from right under him.

Governor Thomas Rogers was surely succumbed by intense fear and bothersome worry at this point in time, because of that menacing cop pitted against him called Commander Robert Stewart. He thought to himself: holy shit. If Robert Stewart suddenly tells everyone that I'm beating my wife, and this goes out publicly, imagine the fucking scandal against me. It will certainly be detrimental to my political career. Shit – I can only imagine if everyone in the public knows that I, Governor Thomas Rogers is a scum-sucking wife basher! Fucking hell, can you imagine what would happen to me and my reputation if this ever hits the newspapers!

Henceforth, Governor Thomas Rogers understood the very equally serious and dire consequences and repercussions of having Robert Stewart now coming against him as a fervent enemy! And all Thomas Rogers was able to do at present was cancel any day's press conferences and stay at home in solitude, and just fucking worry. And so, the sorry excuse of a governor just spent the entire day feeling anxious, preoccupied in overthinking rants going over and over inside his head of what Robert Stewart was planning to do to him next.

Governor Thomas Rogers understood that Robert Stewart was a very dangerous enemy. And now that Robert Stewart had him in his sights, he was certainly scared to death of what that police commander had up his sleeve against him next. Because he understood that Robert Stewart would not want a wife-bashing corrupt governor heading the State in any political capacity whatsoever, especially functioning in high office, particularly running the State of New York as Governor himself. So, as a nasty consequence, Governor Thomas Rogers understood one thing was definite, one outcome to the confrontation he just had with Robert Stewart - and that was unmistakably: Robert Stewart is going to come after me with all his might - and that bastard menacing police commander is not going to stop until he not only stripped me-Governor Thomas Rogers of my precious title and my political career, but Robert Stewart's intention was to quite simply put me-Thomas Rogers into the ground once and for all and permanently!

Meanwhile, Thomas Rogers kept preoccupied with that thought throughout the entire day, whilst he cancelled all political functions and remained inside his New York State Executive Mansion in Albany, confined inside his study room office in perfect solitude, succumbed by anxious thoughts and one fucking hell of derived, mind-coiling mad scenarios defining or redefining his constant and unhelped state of worry.

Thomas Rogers thought of Robert Stewart as he sat down on his leather armchair behind his wooden desk; the governor literally sweating and fearfully panicking: Damn you, Robert Stewart. Your physical and spiritual powers are insane. And after that confrontation with you earlier last night, you have really got me low-key fucking scared of you! Yours, Robert Stewart, is an authority that is mysterious without defining words. Your intelligence is truly intimidating. And despite the facades I put in public, you have got me scared out of my fucking wits as to your ability to see through people like me. Yes. I have to admit this only to myself. The fear and the panic, the fucking state of panic I'm experiencing of almighty Robert Stewart is truly a confession of my guilt that I have, due to the many crimes I have committed, many coverups of serious felons in this state - and the sort of terrible creature that I truly am, hiding behind the mask, the political nice guy mask of caring and concerned New York Governor title.

I know you, Robert Stewart. I know you as everyone else in the Criminal Kingdom knows you. You notice things that escape the detection of everybody else! You can see through bullshit just like a fucking X-ray machine into a human body can detect the tiniest cancerous growth mass forming. You saw corruption in my public smile before anyone else could even suspect that my character was shady and diabolical. And I knew you felt something was off in the energy I exuded publicly, even long before our recent confrontation earlier in the darkness. I knew you smelled a rat a mile away. I also knew you could penetrate my thoughts and my character and see the truth behind what I was always projecting, my hollow and empty words. You could also read everything between the lines. You could read through what I was not saying as opposed to the lies and the facades and the pretences of what I was saying. The problem with you Robert Stewart, is that you read too many truths into people like me that everyone else conveniently ignores for my benefit. And I know your cunning, strategic approach. You keep your true thoughts of me hidden and to yourself. You investigate first and establish solid evidence matching your true-to-life suspicions of people like me, before you broadcast everything you know about my shady character and criminal actions hiding behind a mask and a title that I wear as governor of New York!

I don't know how you do it Robert Stewart. You have this uncanny, unexplainable internal discipline of silence, watching and waiting and amassing necessary clues, truths and evidence before you strike against your targets. And now I know in painstaking fear, yes, I know Robert Stewart, that right now you are targeting me. And you are targeting me Commander Robert Stewart, not just by your previous suspicions I know you always had of me, but now you are targeting me in even greater degrees, because you know the truth that I am a worthless, useless, wife-bashing piece of shit of a governor of New York! These are the thoughts that keep rising in my mind in silence as I sit inside my study room contemplating everything to myself, such nonsense. Correction…it is not fucking nonsense… It is the fucking truth. And the real fucking truth is that I know you know these damning truths about me Commander Robert Stewart. And I also know that it's only a matter of time before you hang me with those truths Commander Robert Stewart!

I know what you're thinking right now Commander Robert Stewart. I know! I really fucking know!!! Man, you think that you have a piece of shit as a governor of this state. That's what you think, isn't it Commander Robert Stewart? You truly believe, you truly think, you downright fucking know that I-ME, your Governor Thomas Rogers is a true fucking piece of shit! That's what you're thinking about me, isn't it Commander Robert Stewart? OK, OK, OK. It's not a question. It's a fucking testimony! Your testimony Police Commander Robert Stewart.

You are truly trained as a high-calibre cop by mighty forces - and you had developed your skills of perception and seeing through bullshit by a force that cannot be comprehended at all by any normal person. And that makes me truly uncomfortable! That awareness of yours certainly makes people truly shit bricks and piss painful nails! Your perception and your awareness are operating at intelligence levels that no other person in your profession has managed to ever reach. And it's truly scary! I know you are planning something catastrophic against me Commander Robert Stewart! And the fact that I am in the dark about it, I don't know what it is you are planning, is certainly consuming me from head to foot with unimaginable fears at present! I know you're gonna come after me Commander Robert Stewart. But for the life of me, I don't know when and I don't know how! I just know what I know about you Commander Robert Stewart - and it's truly frightening me! Your discipline and your restraint, your silence and perception are true qualities that bring about all your targets' demises! Every time you make a silent revelation about people like me, it only defines your true powers to the world of criminals such as myself, in awe-inspiring chaos! You plant yourself in the shadows and you watch and you study people's hidden motives and hidden secret words never spoken, and you make your determinations and come to your correct conclusions. You expertly strip off masks of people's facades, at the same time as you secretly gather evidence to hang your prey, full stop! That's what you're planning against ME now, isn't it Commander Robert Stewart?

You're planning to bring about the death and destruction, downfall and ruination of I-me, the governor of New York, isn't that right Police Commander Robert Stewart? You want to destroy me, don't you Robert Stewart? You wanna crush me under your feet like a bug, don't you Commander Robert Stewart? You really don't care about my title, do you Robert

Stewart? My title does not intimidate you at all, does it Commander Robert Stewart? You don't give a fuck who I am and what I'm called, do you Commander Robert Stewart? You just gonna come after me like a loose cannon, much like a fucking speeding train that has veered off its tracks! You really want to crush and smash me into the walls, into the ground, don't you Police Commander Robert Stewart!!! And I do use exclamation marks after that last question, because I know it's not really a fucking question at all, it's a fucking statement, with exclamation marks attached to it! I fucking know you, Commander Robert Stewart. I'm really not that dumb to ask questions when the answers are fucking obvious. And I…I'm proclaiming to you Commander Robert Stewart, that I'm really not that fucking dumb, despite what you think about me, Police Commander Robert Stewart!

I know that every thought you predicted about me is just an uncomfortable truth! And you thought about that in silence, didn't you Police Commander Robert Stewart! Again, it's not a fucking question. It's a fucking statement with a fucking exclamation mark attached to the end of it! Yes. Whilst I could fool the whole public with nice words and a nice guy image, such public flocked to me to listen to my comfortable stories and my comfortable words, when I told them that I had their best interests in mind. But not you Commander Robert Stewart! No. No. Not you, Commander Robert Stewart. I fucking know you Commander Robert Stewart too - and I know that you were listening to my false words and my false speeches, whilst I was certainly fooling the rest of the New York Community, but I never fooled you, did I Police Commander Robert Stewart? No. I never fucking fooled you at all did I, Police Commander Robert Stewart? No, not at all. Because all my false words and false proclamations and falsehood lies and scams that I was speaking publicly, you had unravelled into specific truths, which identified my true character of fake, phoney and fraudulent words and criminal actions I was committing against the people behind all their backs, whilst hiding those phoney words and corrupt actions through a pretence I was putting across to everyone of being nice.

But…but you saw right through me from the very beginning. You understood the truth about me, didn't you Police Commander Robert Stewart, right from the get-go! Yes, Robert Stewart. I most definitely understand the truth about you and how you operate painfully clearly. I know that your perception skills are not going to conveniently switch off for my benefit, just because I wear the title which I never deserved to wear, which is New York Governor!

But I concealed my facade quite cunningly and very cleverly to the public. All of them…so many people are just dumb. But then…then I came to realise that just as I can fool 99 out of 100 people, there is always that one bastard amongst people like me in the Criminal Kingdom, who cannot be fooled. And dare I say that name again. Dare I say the name, Commander Robert Stewart. You are one name, one curse, one anomaly – and one freakish spook story that cannot be denied, that cannot be manipulated, that cannot be fooled, that cannot be lied to and tricked, much in contrast unlike everybody else, who can be lied to, manipulated, tricked and fooled in a world of imbeciles, idiots and fucking dumbshits!

Oh… Oh indeed, how I curse the name Robert Stewart right now! That freakish name and that scary spook story cannot be denied any further! What do I do now I ask myself? What can I do now, I ask myself constantly and constantly and constantly again? I must come up with the answers of how to deal with you Commander Robert Stewart.

You see the way I figure it; I have to do you in before you do me in, Police Commander

Robert Stewart! Do you know what really bugs me about you Commander Robert Stewart? It's that you have this uncanny ability of seeing through people like me and people like me can never see through you. You are a mystery, a true mystery, an enigma. I cannot read your mind. I don't know what you are thinking about me. You know every fucking bit of your bad thoughts about me. BUT - I don't know what you are thinking about me, I don't know what you are planning against me. And that is what is causing me, my fucking being, a lot of anxious thoughts and terrible feelings rising inside of me.

Because what I do know is that you are thinking very negative thoughts about me and planning very destructive actions to bring about my downfall and ruination at this very moment. But I cannot predict the exact intricate details of all your thoughts and all your actions you are plotting and scheming against me right this very second! I know you can read me like a piece of poo on the ground, but for the life of me, I cannot read you. And I cannot dissect your exact thoughts and your exact actions you have in store for me! You wanna kill me, don't you Police Commander Robert Stewart? Is it really a question or should I have attached another exclamation mark after it, at the end of that question, which is in fact not a question at all, but a fucking statement with an exclamation mark that should be attached to the end of it.

You really want to kill me, don't you, Police Commander Robert Stewart! Well, guess what, Police Commander Robert Stewart? I wanna kill you as well! And yes indeed, Robert Stewart, I will most certainly plan to kill you!

You see, Commander Robert Stewart, I know that you know most people like me do not live in truth. No, not at all! We live in perfectly arranged facades and public stories that conceal such facades! And I also know Robert Stewart that your entire presence threatens those perfect facades and nice guy stories that people like me spray in all directions to a very gullible and a very foolish public community, that listens and believes what politicians like me say, much to their detriments! And I also know about the very serious and dangerous repercussions to your knowing Robert Stewart. Not only do you see through my facades, but you are also planning to attack me because of such facades! When I give a speech to the public, my words come off as innocent, but you see through every word I speak, and you use those words as a motive to come after me and expose me - and to bring about my ending in high office as governor of New York!

I portray a mask of confidence to the public, but I know with your uncanny perception skills and your see-through-brick-wall eyesight, you diagnose my confidence as an insecurity of mine. You diagnose my nice words as a dirty man hiding a lot of dirty skeletons!

When I claimed to the public that I care, I know you can see through the true opposite meaning to my words, Commander Robert Stewart, as your bullshit detector inside your brain determines that my clean words are truly unclean, and my nice guy image is truly hiding a lot of dirty secrets in the shadows. You dissect words, patterns and determine hidden motives to such a frightening degree, that would rival any detective equivalent of a Sherlock Holmes investigative mindset - and law enforcement analytical brain, comprising of the most stubborn detective reasoning! You outmatch them all Commander Robert Stewart! You certainly have no equal in the field of law enforcement see-through-dog-crap and hidden motivations of the most complicated facade people like me wear in front of everybody else in the entire world! Can I hide anything from you, Police Commander Robert Stewart? I truly suspect not! Your bloody mind! Your bloody eyesight! Your bloody detective presence plunged within our midst much like a curse, a catastrophe, waiting to bring about the doom and gloom of all pretences and all hypocrisies, threatening to bring truth to all lies and revelations to all falsehoods!

Oh, how I hate your presence being amongst my domain, Police Commander Robert Stewart! Oh, the discomfort, the intense discomfort you have instilled in every fibre of my criminal bones! I can fool everyone but the fact that I cannot fool you Police Commander Robert Stewart is certainly going to be the death and destruction, downfall and ruination of me, if I do not manage to kill you first, Police Commander Robert Stewart! The fact that your awareness picks up home truths that I otherwise expertly keep hidden, is what truly unnerves me and makes me uncomfortable Robert Stewart! It unnerves me a great deal! I know that every hypocritical speech I give is dissected by you, whereby you see behind those words of what I am presenting to my fellow stupid constituents! All of a sudden because of what you can see through me, I've developed a nervous laughter. My words are hesitant, but I feel myself overexplaining, even in your absence, as if you are standing right before me… I'm already becoming defensive, ready to answer all those questions that I know eventually you're gonna throw in my direction. Or I fear you will ask… But I'm already preparing to overexplain myself and defend myself, even before you confront me again and ask me any further questions of my guilt in any subject, I know you are accusing me of…

And this is how clever you really are Commander Robert Stewart. In your presence, people have a nasty habit of revealing themselves even before you interrogate them. Because of the very uncomfortable pressure you put on people when you accurately perceive them as a piece of shit, is something that people like me cannot take any longer. You apply pressure Robert Stewart that shatters all egos and makes people like me slip.

What's hidden is revealed even by the own mouths, and very own admissions of felons as your governor of New York, Thomas Rogers. Me…yes me, Commander Robert Stewart! You don't need to break someone's false stories during any interrogation to determine the truth. Your solemn understanding of people like me as born bullshit artists weakens any efforts and attempts that we have to shield that truth from you! Your accuracy is always on point. You see the cracks in our armour just by perception and just by simply fucking 'knowing!' Because the foundation of your existence Robert Stewart exudes a radar that dismantles and exposes each piece of shit scandalous hidden flaw of reality residing throughout our entire sordid beings, revealing all the dark truths into the cores of our characters, even before you ask any questions! You are a multi-layered man Commander Robert Stewart, who holds multiple truths into multiple subjects, just by uncanny instinct and unwavering perception. And that is why I fear I can never hide anything from you, Commander Robert Stewart. And I equally fear your next attacks planned against me by your destructive hands. And that is why I must come up with a contingency plan to truly dismantle your forecasted attacks and get rid of you, once and for all, finally, before I know you are eventually going to get rid of me if I do not remove you from circulation quickly and efficiently!

Your detective skills bring a distinctive nuance into your field of policing and law enforcement. You see through illusions as if people like me are confiding in you. And because you can do that, I feel complete and totally destabilised at present! Your life is disruptive and destructive to my plans of serving the rich and making money from those rich people I serve and protect. Your mind operates at a different level of frequency to others. And you are quite, simply put, a genuinely high-risk presence that is extremely dangerous to illusions.

People like me in the past have always underestimated you, Commander Robert Stewart. We mostly misconstrued you and we even misread you. And you know the results of that fundamental error, fatal flaw, crash-landing epic fuck up, foolish bungles and gross miscalculation and tragic failures of our judgments… It results in costing us everything… Every time we underestimate you Robert Stewart, it ends up costing us everything…everything we built, including the very structure of our lives succumbs to dismantling crumbs and ruinous ashes! You are a destroyer Commander Robert Stewart! Everything you touch not only gets exposed but henceforth explodes. The Criminal Kingdom is damned because of you, Police Commander Robert Stewart. Your awareness is what is truly disruptive to our plans, Police Commander Robert Stewart.

If it wasn't for you bad copper, I would have no problem getting away with how I portray myself to the public and to politics in general in New York and the entire United States of America. I would be able to fool everyone. I would be able to get away with accepting bribes in exchange for protecting wealthy sinister beings operating out into the community. All of us would remain untouchable by the people that we can fool into continuing to vote for us, and also we would all remain untouched by every fibre of the law, the very law you are policing, Commander Robert Stewart, if you were not operating within the walls of the judicial process, serving against us, and seeing through what everyone else in the community constantly remains in the dark to such truths and realities, that people like me hide from them quite cunningly and quite expertly at each turn for years on end… But…but right now we can't hide anything because of a dreadful threat like you is in existence, Commander Robert Stewart.

We cannot get away with anything because you Commander Robert Stewart happen to be painstakingly in the picture dissecting us from both, near and from afar… You are seeing the inner depths of rubbish that is usually disguised in a clean suit and a clean tie… You are pointing your damning fingers at people like me who are wearing respectable titles, such as governor of New York. And in your mind, you are saying, this man is dirty! This man is a criminal pretending to be clean! You are saying that this man is hiding very sinister secrets through his words of false proclamations and pretentious niceties portrayed through two-faced hypocritical speeches, spoken before a dim-witted, ignorant public community! You are calling us stink bomb lepers, as we walk with our heads tall, smiling in public, wearing our expensive freshly ironed suits. You are constantly looking at us sideways, Commander Robert Stewart! You are constantly judging us, Commander Robert Stewart… And dare I say, you are judging us accurately. Because I am your governor, Commander Robert Stewart - and I revealed to myself that I am an extremely corrupt politician who has the community's worst interests in mind. I am currently accepting gifts and tokens of friendship by one of the worst mass murderers that New York has ever seen, called Amir Hamza. And Amir Hamza is one of the dirtiest felons and mass murderers in the history of New York, whose Big Pharma Corporation or Enterprise has been responsible for killing masses upon masses of sick people in this country and others, who are prescribed his deadly-manufactured drugs.

I am protecting this man Commander Robert Stewart. That is what I know. That is what I've kept hidden from the public. But I know Commander Robert Stewart that I cannot keep these truths hidden from you… I know you're planning to get me for these home truths Commander Robert Stewart! I know, I know everything about you Commander Robert Stewart… But do you know, do you really know Police Commander Robert Stewart, that I am planning your death and removal from circulation very shortly, before you are able to succeed in finagling my downfall and destruction at any moment, as I am thinking what I am thinking in connection to you, Commander Robert Stewart???

You must understand Commander Robert Stewart, that I, Thomas Rogers, Governor of New York, has no other recourse but to plot your death. You know I have no choice, don't you Commander Robert Stewart! Because as long as you are around targeting me, my mind will be permanently consumed with improper mechanisms of anxious thoughts. And everything that I built will just simply not last. Because by your presence alone, I feel the walls around me are crumbling! I have no other choice, no recourse but to act in a manner I must. I must permanently remove that threat of your existence from my political sphere, period! I will not sit back and watch you dismantle everything I have achieved in my career Commander Robert Stewart. I will not allow you to destroy me, Commander Robert Stewart. I will put an end once and for all to your cold arrogance that you demonstrate against me! You will not push me off my high office political platform! I will not give up my voice. I will not give up my power, position and autonomy. I will not let you take anything from me that I've spent years building in my career, Commander Robert Stewart! You will not suffocate the life out of me! You will not end me, Commander Robert Stewart!

You think you are going to collapse me under the weight of my own lies? Justice: - is that what you call your actions against me? I cannot tolerate your Divine Justice, Commander Robert Stewart

You are pressure Commander Robert Stewart. You are a lot of pressure to people like me. And your entire existence has only functioned to bring about a hell of a lot of anxiety in certain people. Meaning, ME! Your governor of New York that you have right now treated very disrespectfully! Yes. You are certainly pressure! Barging in to my residence here in Albany and threatening me, as if you are holding a gun ready to shoot me dead right inside this very spot at point-blank range! The balls on you Commander Robert Stewart is insufferable! And because of the pressure and the anxiety that you have caused me, I am currently plotting your death with Amir Hamza, who has requested my services and my counsel to assist in your demise Commander Robert Stewart! We'll see how good you really are Commander Robert Stewart! We will see if you are able to predict and prevent the successful termination of your life, before you are able to sleep another peaceful night again?

CHAPTER 8

Three nights later, New York Governor Thomas Rogers and Big Pharma CEO Amir Hamza hired a hitman to kill Robert Stewart.

They all met up inside the personal study room area of the governor's residence at the New York State Executive Mansion in Albany. The governor and the Big Pharma CEO met up secretly inside the governor's study alone with the hitman present, not knowing the hitman was really Officer Paul Stewart in disguise, with a long black wig and dark sunglasses.

Officer Paul Stewart volunteered for the task to operate as an undercover police official during this assignment, to disguise himself as the perfect hit man, assuming a fake identity and an appropriate disguise, attending the meeting that evening at 10:00 PM sharp, wearing a long, black-coloured trench coat, blending in with these criminal mass murderers quite convincingly.

Officer Paul Stewart posed himself as a dreadful killer for hire willing, able and quite ready to carry out the illicit illegal crime of murdering a police commander for the sole purpose of assisting, behind the scenes,

Commander Robert Stewart to gather the necessary evidence to arrest the criminal parties plotting to hire a hit man, to do murder on a police officer. Paul Stewart of course assumed a false identity to avoid detection whilst infiltrating the criminal office of the New York Governor Thomas Rogers, to get close to monitoring him and his criminal associates, such as Big Pharma King Amir Hamza, to help the New York City Police Department solidify their downfalls expeditiously! And Paul Stewart had the correct physical appearance, clothing and accessories to disguise himself as the perfect stereotype of a hired gun. His very hip mannerisms and speech patterns were very convincing to those evil creatures hiring him to do the case of murder.

And Paul Stewart blended in his role and disguise with the corrupt governor and the corrupt big pharma billionaire perfectly and convincingly, not only ensuring his safety, but his effectiveness in gathering all the necessary evidence to have the governor and the big pharma chief executive officer finally stopped dead in their tracks, ending their criminal reigns against the people of New York and the United States of America as a whole! Paul Stewart established their trust quite proficiently - and now as he was invited inside the governor's den with Amir Hamza, they began discussing illegal activities, such as what Paul as a disguised hitman was being paid to perform: the murder of Police Commander Robert Stewart!

Officer Paul Stewart's assumed identity and alias whilst posing as a hitman was Crimson Ghost. He even smiled jokingly to the two corrupt fiends comprising of the governor and big pharma tycoon hiring him, and equally sharing in the expense of his payment, that his surname 'Ghost' befitted his particular skills of murder. He explained that after he killed his victims, he vanished much like a ghost avoiding detection wherever he went, even making it sound uncontrived! He carried out the perfect set up! And of course, Robert Stewart was hidden in close by proximity to the scene, as necessary back up with police cavalry, watching and listening through his cleverly planted surveillance devices that were hidden inside the executive mansion's premises!

And before long, the discussions commenced. The governor and the big pharma chief executive officer initiated their dreadful conversations to Paul Stewart concerning his task of doing murder in great detail!

The governor explained to his hired gun Crimson Ghost, "I want Commander Robert Stewart dead as soon as possible. Even if you have to go to his house when he is home, knock on the door, and when he answers the door, just point your weapon and blast him to pieces. Whatever it takes! But I want him out of my life, because I am scared to death of that man and what he is planning against me. That son of a bitch cop Robert Stewart is a one-man army. I know he is planning something big to destroy me. But I will not allow him. I will simply destroy him first! Now that my wife has left me because of Robert Stewart anything is possible. When she left me in Robert Stewart's presence, she had special red welts (bruises) on her face from my striking hands. And I know Robert Stewart is planning something very big and very dangerous to bring about my downfall! But I will not let that happen. I will destroy Robert Stewart before he has a chance to destroy me! And that is where you come into the picture my very good friend, Crimson Ghost! You will kill Robert Stewart as soon as possible and very quickly, so that I can finally escape the horrible fate he has in store for me!"

The man known as Crimson Ghost nodded his head slightly at the words and remarked in his disguised voice, "I will do as you ask, Sir!"

Amir Hamza spoke next the following words, "I too want Robert Stewart gone. I cannot have Robert Stewart snooping around in my business and figuring out that my created pharmaceutical drugs have resulted in masses of murders of doctors' patients in this city, this country and this entire globe, where I sell my manufactured goods to accordingly. I don't want Robert Stewart around to expose me either!"

Crimson Ghost again nodded his head, giving them both convincing but in himself (fake) assurances once again that he would carry out his task they hired him to perform extremely successfully.

Amir Hamza explained to Crimson Ghost that he was CEO and majority shareholder in a pharmaceutical company called, Hamza Inc. Amir Hamza also explained himself and his various titles he went by, calling himself labels such as: King, CEO, Tycoon or Billionaire. But Paul Stewart knew the real truth. Amir Hamza was truly a genocidal lunatic responsible for killing many people through his pharmaceutical drug-manufacturing business!

Paul Stewart understood immediately that Amir Hamza was also scared of the repercussions of Commander Robert Stewart's life, posing a great risk and lethal hazard to his existence, through Robert's investigations that shone a very bright light into his big pharma company and diabolical activities, showing that Hamza was involved in conspiracies of acting in dangerously secretive and viciously sinister ways, that harmed and killed patients, through the availability of drug-created medications which imposed deadly side effects to all those people prescribed such lethal drugs under the false proviso, that those drugs were helping them. But that simply was not true. The drugs given to them by Big Pharma Chief Executive Officer Amir Hamza had certainly resulted in their deaths! And that was what Amir Hamza was trying to cover up also, by hiring him-Crimson Ghost to do away with Robert, to protect himself from prosecution, just as the governor wanted Crimson Ghost to murder Robert, so they could both protect themselves from Robert's ongoing investigations into their illegal activities, thus bringing about their downfalls!

Amir Hamza explained in his deep voice and Middle Eastern accent, "If Robert Stewart is not made dead quickly, he will prove my unethical practises within the pharmaceutical industry, whereby my drugs are run with misleading marketing campaigns, that are oddly for the sole purpose of money-making profits, at the expense of patients' welfare and lives. Robert Stewart will also uncover the dubiousness involved in monopolizing the industry via price manipulations of my drugs, so that I can make a lot of money from their sales to global markets in the pharmaceutical industry, at the same time as attempting to drive others out of the business. Robert Stewart will also uncover that I'm involved in bribery; that I in fact am bribing the governor of New York, who in turn, is protecting me and shielding me from prosecution. NOW – given all that, if Robert Stewart is left alive any longer, he will also uncover that me-myself and the governor hired you Crimson Ghost to assassinate him-Robert Stewart! Of course you can see, I am sure you can appreciate, that we cannot permit that to happen. So, I insist…I fucking demand that Robert Stewart must be disposed of at once! I'm sure my governor friend here concurs with me!"

The governor nodded his head at them both, agreeing with Amir Hamza's words, full stop! And the man known as Crimson Ghost also nodded his head, that he would do away with Robert Stewart rather quickly. Both the governor and Amir Hamza were quite satisfied in Crimson Ghost's spoken rhetoric and oratory style to the affirmative - and they expressed confidence in his abilities to do away with their target, not only efficiently, but successfully, at whatever cost!

The governor further explained to Crimson Ghost, "You want to know a crazy secret about fear?" He said referring to his immense terror of Police Commander Robert Stewart. The Governor Thomas Rogers went on. "Fear is when a man like Commander Robert Stewart has no regard for a high office title such as my own, and he waltzes on inside my residence here and starts threatening me, resulting in my heart skipping many beats. Robert Stewart personally shows to me his true power and I have to tell you Mr Crimson Ghost, that that reality had truly frightened me! He showed me no restraint, no respect and no acknowledgement of my high-office stature as governor of New York. He just stormed inside here with his sick arse some nights ago and took my wife from me at the same time as he pointed his authoritative finger at my face, at point-blank range, and threatened me, giving me horrible firm orders to stay away from my wife. That is one man I don't want around me ever again.

"This man makes my inner circle, my alliances, even my family irrelevant, just through his presence alone! Who can tolerate such a dreadful, intimidating, threatening character to exist in society one second longer? I know I surely can't! My title as governor couldn't crack one ounce of regard for me. He completely dismissed everything I am and just walked all over me. Can you believe the nerve of that man? He stomped into this house and treated me as if I am some punk on the street. He talked to me as if I am some low-life junkie. When instead, he was talking to the governor of New York. But he tossed aside everything I am and everything I am labelled as and just treated me like shit in my own home right here. What an insufferable fucking arsehole Commander Robert Stewart truly is. What a nasty motherfucker that guy is, to have no regard and no respect for a man in my position of power and influence throughout the state of New York! Who the fuck does he think he is?

"I'm not trying to justify my actions in hiring you Crimson Ghost to terminate him. I just want you to understand who we are dealing with. Because I want you to make the task of his murder all the more painful. To punish him for treating me the way he treated me inside my house a few nights ago! I want you to make him suffer before he dies! That man is the sole personification of chaos. And when he confronted me, I was lucky I didn't drop dead right then and there from a fucking heart attack. When Robert Stewart confronted me the other night, I truly understood what sort of an enemy I am really dealing with who is called Commander Robert Stewart. I realised then and there, that Robert Stewart's life only secures our failures. I realised at that horrible moment, that I was not going to allow that man, that damn cop to ever make me feel that way again. So, when my associate Amir Hamza approached me a couple nights ago to assist him in doing away with Robert Stewart, I wholeheartedly agreed in his plan - and was much willing to participate in that grand goal to execute Robert Stewart without a crumb of hesitation!

"Robert Stewart certainly exudes darkness. And it is that darkness that scares the living shit out of me! But I will show that bastard cop what darkness really is, when I send my hired gun you Crimson Ghost after him, to do away with him slowly, painfully - but effectively! All my years in political life I thought that the secrecy of what I truly stood for gave me power and autonomy. But because of Robert Stewart, I'm unable to keep any of my fucking secrets under wraps! Robert Stewart's presence alone shines a light on every incriminating dirty word and every incriminating evil action that I've spoken and committed throughout my entire existence! Commander Robert Stewart's entire existence shakes the very foundations of our existences, by smashing illusions and revealing truths that people like me want kept hidden! And let me tell you something, not only am I scared of Robert Stewart's strength, but I am absolutely terrified of his determination to throw me into the trash and let my corpse rot away. His arrogance is irritating. His confidence in his abilities against people like me is a violent indictment against me, that spells that I have already lost this battle between me and Robert Stewart! Every word I speak, every action I conspire, becomes a mandate, a proclamation Robert Stewart utilises against me, to have me hanged! No matter what I do and try to keep hidden, Robert Stewart's presence is a very catalyst that exposes all secrets and brings to light everything shady! Robert Stewart's brilliance against people like me is not just coincidence, it's fucking consequence!

"Even before the war between us began, Robert Stewart's aura had outranked my precious title as governor. Robert Stewart has no respect and no regard for hierarchy. He just calls a spade a spade. He'll just come after you even if he sniffs something foul in our odors! I have never faced a man like that who calls raising hell his favourite pastime. That man's survival has defied the criminal kingdom's darkness and expectations for too long. He talks with power and endurance, and even turns me, the governor of New York into experiencing feelings of guilt and confusion! After I met his damning presence in my home a few nights ago, I could never eat and never sleep from that point on. But…but my mind began losing focus and my concentration was constantly drifting! I tried to control my wife and make her obedient to me, but because of Robert Stewart, all my attempts had backfired! He took that piece of vagina out of my house and now I'm left with nothing but bad thoughts and bad memories – and a bitter urge of wanting Robert Stewart dead, for all the misery his brief encounter with me was responsible for causing me! His encounter with me was brief, but goddamn it, I have to fucking tell you people, that that horrible confrontation left a lasting impression on me. He has truly scarred me for life. My thoughts are now becoming twisted nightmares, whereby his threatening face is forever imprinted in my psyche!

"Not only has Robert Stewart made me feel exposed, but despite my title as governor of New York, he made me feel irrelevant. He made me feel small, very small. His horrible presence alone has made my position as governor obsolete and my power in this state of New York a dragnet, a very trap of quicksand he has sunk me in!

"Robert Stewart has mastered the battleground to win victory against all obstacles and ignore the phoney titles which people like me wear as masks. He just charges ahead treating everyone equally, whilst sparing no name, no title and no human being, no matter what position of power they think they have to his unmerciful wrathful justice! He entered my house a few nights ago and saw through the facade instantly. He uncovered the secret chaos and exposed everything that resides inside this mansion of mine. As soon as he entered this house, he understood from the first second, that this entire building was drenched in lies, corruption, manipulation and every form of hypocrisy. He determined all of that, not through so many words spoken, but I knew what he knew about me that second... Because his very shadow spoke indirect connotations on his behalf which informed me: I know what you are even though I will not tell you right now. I've uncovered all your dirty skeletons, and I know where all the bodies are buried, you sham of a governor!

"He entered my den of deceit and somehow, he got into my head and I began confessing, spilling my guts to him through some unexplainable brainwave of self-incriminating damning revelations! That is the mysterious power of Robert Stewart! And that is why I want Robert Stewart dead immediately. Because where he is concerned, he has filled my entire being with hate and horror! And the terror that he has caused me, has spread to every part of my being from head to foot, much like an infection!"

CHAPTER 9

As soon as the corrupt New York Governor Thomas Rogers finished spilling his guts to his hired assassin Crimson Ghost, Amir Hamza quickly revealed his true diabolical side, in a rapid twist, to his very dark and sinister character.

The maid entered the private den holding a feather duster, prepared to do some cleaning unannounced, when Amir Hamza jumped towards her in a volatile and unplanned reaction, grabbed her, then placed one arm around her neck savagely. This intense violent action startled Officer Paul Stewart in disguise as Crimson Ghost, when Amir Hamza immediately shouted at Paul the following orders, "I want to test you Mr. Crimson Ghost. I want to know that you are as capable as you say you are… I want to know if you are truly able to accomplish the task we have set before you and paid you for, you know the first initial part payment for the assassination of Commander Robert Stewart. So, to prove to us that you are able to kill him, I want you to first kill this maid in front of us."

Paul Stewart was not surprised by such an order and hideous task being presented to him by Amir Hamza. Paul understood quite well the diabolical monster dark man this big pharma chief executive officer exuded in every fibre of his being. But what had quietly startled Paul at present was the fact that the governor of New York did not seem concerned the least that one of his faithful maids, who worked for the governor's office for over two years would right then and there become sacrificed for murder, for the sole purpose of testing the hired gun Crimson Ghost's would-be notorious abilities to effectively and efficiently commit murder.

Paul Stewart in himself much quietly had an even lower opinion of the governor of New York Thomas Rogers right this very minute than previously experienced prior his undercover role as a hired killer for the two criminal unconscionable mass murderers, who went by the names, Thomas Rogers and Amir Hamza.

That lowdown, rotten, stinking, fucking son of a bitch governor, Paul Stewart thought to himself in secrecy. That scum Governor Thomas Rogers was willing to kill one of his loyal people, his own maid, just to prove a point right now. There were no depths of evil that the governor would not stoop to. And this maid was not only loyal and faithful to her governor and previous (mostly sacked) governor predecessors before Thomas Rogers, now working for the New York Governor's Office for over two years, but this poor sweet maid who was an attractive woman in her late twenties, and what was even more devastating to her life being threatened right now by the governor and his aiding-and-abetting accomplice Amir Hamza, was the fact that this maid was four months pregnant. During his investigation into the governor and his associates, Paul Stewart gathered all the information of not only the governor and Amir Hamza, but all those who worked for the governor, including this maid who was four months pregnant in her late twenties.

And now the governor was willing to kill her and her unborn child inside her at a whim, just merely by the suggestion of having her death used to pass a test, orchestrated by Amir Hamza. And the governor of New York Thomas Rogers went along with it very easily with no hesitation, no emotion and no remorse, rather unconscionably, willing to risk her life and have her killed together with her unborn child unexpectedly and wilfully, as one stupid fucking test.

Paul Stewart kept the shock he felt inside of him to himself, which was caused rather ferociously by being asked to kill this precious maid and her unborn child quite unexpectedly in a rather brutal surprising turn of events unfolding before his eyes at this point in time. Paul Stewart already proved himself to be a professional law-enforcement official. He handled himself extremely well under even the most intense pressure his police profession had subjected him to at any given time, with no warning, as the surprise of his life was thrown in his face at this very moment!

Paul Stewart looked at the terrified maid being restrained by Amir Hamza's firm grip, his arm gripped tightly around her neck, squeezing into her throat and blocking her screams, and quite possibly, almost choking her. Paul Stewart saw the frightened panic in her eyes. Her voice was blocked from speaking. But Paul Stewart could read her mind. She knew if she was able to talk, she would say, don't kill me, I am pregnant.

Paul Stewart no longer considered his job to incriminate and imprison the governor as professional any longer. He considered his job very personal and his terrible feelings he was succumbed to at present were extremely unhelped. As a severe consequence right now to his ill feelings, Paul Stewart felt like killing the governor and his scumbag of all scumbag aiding-and-abetting accomplices, called Amir Hamza. But throughout this horrible ordeal, Paul Stewart kept his calm. He kept playing it cool, waiting for an opening to strike at the governor and Amir Hamza before they could cost another person their life right now. Even Paul knew his life was being threatened for murder.

Paul Stewart kept silent when Amir Hamza spoke words in grave tones of a shout, in a much hostile menacingly dangerous manner towards what he considered his hired gun named Crimson Ghost, when he hollered at Crimson Ghost, barking the following words, yelling at him threateningly, telling him in intonations of uncompromising volatile tyrannical demands, "So, you big shot Crimson Ghost… You tell us you can kill Robert Stewart… Then prove it… You kill this fucking stupid dumb bitch maid right now. After all, she was stupid enough to get herself pregnant, so she will no longer be in the employ of the governor for much longer, because she will have to take time off for her pregnancy. So let us just save ourselves the trouble of having to delay her replacement. I want her killed now. And I want you Crimson Ghost to kill her, to prove to us, to me-Amir Hamza and the governor of New York Thomas Rogers, that you are able to do a job of murder on this maid proficiently, to show us that you can also accomplish the difficult task we have put in front of you of Robert Stewart's murder! So, you show us right now what you can do, or should I just snap this maid's neck with my bare hands - and order your execution right here and right now at the same time, hey? Come on, you fucking dummy man. I want to see you kill her right now. Because if you fail, I will kill you right here and right this very moment. And at the same time as I fuck your life into the ground and I kill you, I will kill this very fragile slender maid with my hands or my arm around her throat, snapping her neck."

Paul understood that he would have to act quickly in order to save the maid's life and his own life from a double murder, ready to be committed any moment now. But including her unborn child, that meant a triple murder was in progress!

The governor of New York Thomas Rogers now spoke to Paul with the same equally ferocious and callous demeanour, using threatening intensities and demanding voice tones, as his accomplice just hammered into him previously. The governor looked at Paul with evil malicious eyes and hideously sinister intentions, as he then raised his voice and shouted at the man he believed to be called Crimson Ghost, "Come on you fucking assassin. This stupid bitch of a maid here has proven her disloyalty by getting pregnant. So, she will be leaving me shortly. So, I have deemed her life to be over. I will sacrifice her life right now for her treason in getting pregnant and leaving me soon. NOW, I want you Crimson Ghost to kill her right now. Pull out your gun from inside your trench coat, point it to her head and blow her away."

Paul Stewart noticed that Amir Hamza did not present a gun into his hands right now, so he was safe on that score. Although he knew that he always carried a gun concealed beneath his garments. It was only a short matter of seconds before he would grab for it. Paul understood that he would have to act to resolve the situation to his benefit before that happened. But the governor picked up a pair of large scissors from his desk approaching the maid and said, "if you don't kill her right now, I will stab her in her belly and kill her and her unborn child this very fucking second!" Cursed the governor.

Paul Stewart was prepared to act swiftly in his operation of saving the maid, by removing both the criminal sadistic governor and the criminal pharma fraud from circulation in order to accomplish his task rightfully so.

Paul removed the gun pistol from the inside of his trench coat pocket, noticing the governor holding the large dark, blue-coloured scissors approaching the maid, at the same time as Amir Hamza still had his arm around her throat, ready to squeeze and break her neck. Paul thought to himself sourly, that the crazy bastard Amir Hamza wanted him to shoot the maid right between her eyes even as he had his arm around her neck. Amir Hamza was not concerned if the bullet strayed and struck him. Amir Hamza just demanded to Crimson Ghost to fucking shoot her right here and right now!

Paul Stewart steadied the gun in his hand and prepared to fire his revolver accordingly. Amir Hamza was a head taller than the average-sized maid. Therefore, Paul was able to get a good shot at Amir Hamza's head. And by now the governor was one metre away from his intended target, standing at the side of the maid being held in a chokehold by Amir Hamza. The governor was holding the pair of scissors in his hand threatening to kill the maid if Paul Stewart did not shoot her right now.

Paul Stewart understood his task as clear as day and he steadied his aim and prepared to shoot Amir Hamza first, to free the maid from his arm around her throat, ready to break her neck. Paul Stewart got to work quickly. He pointed his gun first pretentiously at the maid - and then in a split of a second, he raised his gun higher than the maid and pointed it quickly between the eyes of Amir Hamza and fired two shots. Amir Hamza fell backwards and the maid was able to struggle herself free to safety from Amir Hamza's clutches. Paul Stewart then quickly turned his gun to the Governor Thomas Rogers, who rapidly darted towards the maid to stab her with the scissors. Paul Stewart swiftly fired another two shots at the side of the governor's head, which instantly resulted in him killing both, Amir Hamza and the governor of New York; two notorious mass murdering bloody criminals then and there at the same time as Paul Stewart saved the life of the startled, weeping maid.

At this time Robert Stewart and his police cavalry stormed the late governor's private den and approached the maid and Paul, concerned for their safeties and much relieved that Paul accomplished his task successfully, saving the maid together with his great life being intact.

Robert shook Paul's hand extremely proud of him. Captain John McCallum was also present and tapped his hand onto Paul's shoulder equally impressed and proud of Paul's great police work in saving the day - and solving the political corruption case the New York City Police Department was heading into the criminal activities of the now Late New York Governor Thomas Rogers.

Robert and John explained to Paul that the police department would cut through the red tape and bureaucracy, whereby Paul would immediately be promoted to 'Detective' upon proving his extreme proficiency and 'Superb' abilities as a police officer, skipping the usual allotted waiting time of such promotions being given to officers upgraded to the greater capacity and official rank of Detective.

Paul regained his normal senses alarmingly rapidly from the ordeal he was just subjected to, and became overjoyed at his older brother's solemn congratulations, even appreciation in assisting them in solving this major criminal case. Paul Stewart immediately returned the handshakes to both Robert and John. And the next time anyone would hear from Paul Stewart in an official police capacity, Paul Stewart would be ranked as Detective Paul Stewart! And the chief commissioner of the 25th division precinct station house of Brooklyn, New York would wholeheartedly sanction the promotion, seeing no reason and no excuse to waste a good police officer as Paul Stewart's talents any longer, by subjecting him to remain as officer. But Paul would now be assisting the police precinct in handling the big murder cases that entered the Police Department officially on all levels!

The next afternoon Robert Stewart received a tip inside the station house on his mobile phone from some mob lackey, he knew was employed by the Armando Family Chieftain. After a screeching-sounding large vehicle that came to a momentary halt outside the 25th division precinct station house took off again, Robert Stewart was contacted on his mobile phone to go outside his police station after the van pulled up and drove off again, to witness the dumped 25 dead bodies outside his station house in broad daylight. The dead bodies comprised of corrupt judges, corrupt politicians, wicked doctors and dishonourable nurses. A second brief phone call conversation claimed to Commander Robert Stewart over his mobile phone, following the lawman witnessing the mass corpses on the pavement outside his police precinct, "No one will stop me from fulfilling my revenge against the scum in this city, especially you, Commander Robert

Stewart. No one will ever stop me! So, prepare yourself for hell on earth to be unleashed in New York City because of what those retarded-arse motherfuckers have done to my family! The dirty judges, the filthy politicians, the corrupt doctors, the corrupt nurses, the corrupt psychologists, the corrupt psychiatrists are going to start dropping dead all throughout the city, right in front of your eyes, my good friend Commander Robert Stewart. For the death of my children, the world is going to pay bitterly. The scum in this city think that they are safe? Those fucking idiots are not safe. No one is safe from me. And no one is immune to my retribution against them! The politicians are being paid to protect the very criminals who have harmed my children. The politicians have taken it upon themselves to harm innocent people as they have harmed my innocent children, which resulted in their deaths. You think that fucking scum governor that you were responsible for putting in the ground ends the corruption in New York? No, my friend Robert Stewart. There are many politicians who are like that fucking scum governor, or should I say, the now dead Governor Thomas Rogers. And there are many people in the medical profession who function like that fucking cunt you police also put in the grave, called Amir Hamza. All politicians are corrupt like Thomas Rogers, and all medical doctors and their counterparts are as dirty and fucking slimy like that piece of shit now dead and buried called Amir Hamza. I want you to understand something: all of them are going to pay! All of them are going to have their blood spilled for what they have done to the members of my family. So, you certainly better be prepared for real hell on earth to be unleashed in New York City. And it will come and no one, not even you Commander Robert Stewart will be able to stop me!!!"

Robert Stewart recognised the voice immediately. The voice was clear as day, without disguises. And the caller called him from a secure untraceable phone as usual. It was homicidal mass murdering maniac, Domenico Armando!

www.ingramcontent.com/pod-product-compliance
Lightning Source LLC
La Vergne TN
LVHW051009080826
845145LV00009B/2532
* 9 7 8 1 9 2 3 6 6 6 3 4 4 *